Love *without* Wings

Also by Louis Auchincloss

FICTION

The Indifferent Children
The Injustice Collectors
Sybil
A Law for the Lion
The Romantic Egoists
The Great World and Timothy Colt
Venus in Sparta
Pursuit of the Prodigal
The House of Five Talents
Portrait in Brownstone
Powers of Attorney
The Rector of Justin
The Embezzler
Tales of Manhattan
A World of Profit
Second Chance
I Come as a Thief
The Partners
The Winthrop Covenant
The Dark Lady
The Country Cousin
The House of the Prophet

The Cat and the King
Watchfires
Narcissa and Other Fables
Exit Lady Masham
The Book Class
Honorable Men
Diary of a Yuppie
Skinny Island
The Golden Calves
Fellow Passengers
The Lady of Situations

NONFICTION

Reflections of a Jacobite
Pioneers and Caretakers
Motiveless Malignity
Edith Wharton
Richelieu
A Writer's Capital
Reading Henry James
Life, Law and Letters
Persons of Consequence: Queen Victoria
and Her Circle
False Dawn: Women in the
Age of the Sun King
The Vanderbilt Era

$\mathcal{L}$OVE
without
$\mathcal{W}$INGS

Some Friendships
in Literature and Politics

LOUIS AUCHINCLOSS

Houghton Mifflin Company

BOSTON · 1991

Library of Congress Cataloging-in-Publication Data

Auchincloss, Louis.
Love without wings : some friendships in literature and politics /
Louis Auchincloss.
p.   cm.
ISBN 0-395-55442-X
1. Great Britain — Biography.   2. United States — Biography.
3. Authors, English — 19th century — Friends and associates.
4. Authors, American — 19th century — Friends and associates.
5. Friendship.   I. Title.
CT119.A87   1991
920.073 — dc20   90-42370
CIP

Printed in the United States of America

HAD   10   9   8   7   6   5   4   3   2   1

Passages from *Holmes-Pollock Letters: The Correspondence of Mr. Justice Holmes and Sir Frederick Pollock, 1874–1932,* edited by Mark DeWolfe Howe (1961), are reprinted by permission of Harvard University Press. Passages from *The Correspondence of Arthur Hugh Clough,* edited by Frederick L. Mulhauser (1957), are reprinted by permission of Oxford University Press. Every effort has been made to obtain permission for use of copyrighted material. Any errors or omissions are unintentional and corrections will be made in future printings if necessary.

For Dick and Starr Lawrence

friends, cousins and neighbors

Friendship is love without his wings!

— Lord Byron

Contents

PREFACE

ANOTHER TITLE for this book might have been *A Disinterested Commerce,* from Oliver Goldsmith's *The Good-Natured Man.* The full quotation is: "Friendship is a disinterested commerce between equals; love an abject intercourse between tyrants and slaves." Any discussion of friendship seems at once to lead to a comparison of it with love between the sexes, not always to the advantage of the latter. But love, for better or worse, certainly receives, in literature as well as life, the greater attention. It is common enough to hear people say that a life without love is hardly worth living. They would be less apt to say it about friendship.

Yet friendship is a quality that we do not share with the other animals. I know this will be disputed by some, but I stick to my guns. Companionship may be open to dogs and cats, and love to certain birds that mate for life, but I do not see how friendship, on any level worth considering, can exist without verbal communication. Friendship is the least physical of human relationships; indeed, at its finest it is not physical at all.

Now this, of course, will be hotly disputed. There are Freudians who will insist that any friendship between two men or two women will of necessity have some physical basis, that there is at least an aspect of homosexuality at the root of all such relationships. I will freely admit that the attraction, conscious or unconscious, between bodies must always have a bearing on friendships; I simply insist that to the extent that this is not so, the friendship will be deeper and truer.

Is friendship limited to partners of the same sex? We know the famous warning in Joyce's *Dubliners,* that love is impossible between man and man because there must *not* be sexual intercourse, and friendship is impossible between man and woman because there must be. But it seems to me that the latter will be true only of persons of excessive libido, or of young people, and by young I mean in their teens. Certainly it need not be true of the elderly or of those in late middle age. Mrs. Winthrop Chanler, in her memoir, *Autumn in the Valley,* says of a Mediterranean cruise with Edith Wharton and four unattached gentlemen, all in their sixties, that it was pleasantly undisturbed by romantic complications. Much of the sexual difficulty in a mixed friendship may be caused by the man's fear of not seeming virile and the woman's that she may have failed to attract. There is no absolute reason that a clear-headed individual should not rise above such misgivings.

Friendship and partnership may become the same thing. Two persons whose capabilities complement each other so as to coalesce into an efficient force to accomplish a particular task are often drawn by shared zeal into strong affection. This seems to have been what brought Harry Hopkins closer to Franklin Roosevelt than any of the President's other assistants in peace or war. If any person, that is, could have been called "close" to FDR. Something similar probably happened between Cardinal Richelieu and his secretary of state, Father Joseph, known as the *éminence grise,* and between Woodrow Wilson and Colonel House, though the latter friendship was ultimately broken up by Mrs. Wilson. Many friendships have been disrupted or destroyed by spouses, particularly wives who felt themselves obscurely threatened by a seemingly excluding intimacy. Husbands in the past were more tolerant of their wives' women friends, presumably because they tended to look down on the other sex and not take its pairings too seriously.

Complementary qualities in two persons need not be associated with a joint task to cement a friendship. They may constitute a happy combination in themselves, what biologists call symbiosis, the intimate living together of two organisms for mutual advantage. John Hay and Henry Adams are an example of this, one outgoing and gregarious but eager not to lose the fruits of solitary study and contemplation, the other distrustful and antisocial but infinitely curious about the goings-on in the great world. Their friendship is perhaps the finest to be examined in this book.

Interdependence, however, must always be a carefully balanced affair, as will be seen in the long relationship between Ivy Compton-Burnett and Margaret Jourdain. If it gets out of balance, it can degenerate into a kind of tyranny, like that of Florence Nightingale, who reduced Arthur Hugh Clough, in Lytton Strachey's biting phrase, to wrapping up brown paper parcels.

Friendship, of course, need not spring from a joint mission or from symbiosis. It may be born of shared tastes — shared exquisite tastes, in the case of Mrs. Chanler and Edith Wharton — or of a loved, shared profession, in the case of Justice Holmes and Sir Frederick Pollock. It may simply grow out of mutual admiration — mutual admiration, in the cases of Byron and Shelley and of Hemingway and Fitzgerald — for each other's art. This last, I should say, constitutes a fragile basis, for it is as often supplemented by jealousy as by love. Friendship may even be the child of nostalgia, growing out of the death of one partner, as with Tennyson and Arthur Hallam, but here it is more fictional than real. And it may result from simple fealty, as with the Princesse de Lamballe and Marie-Antoinette.

What about friendship between rascals? I considered a chapter on Jay Gould and Jim Fisk, but retreated before the probability that Gould, who cheated everybody, even cheated his pal and partner. And even if he had been loyal . . . well, the loyalty of thieves is not an inspiring subject.

Thoreau posited the possibility of friendship among more than two persons, and one's imagination may fly to the Three Musketeers and their motto, One for all and all for one. But this seems to belong more to the category of teams than friends, going back to the instinct of the herd or pack.

Most of us spend a large part of our lives in the company of friends and would feel the loss of much of our sun without them. Yet we tend not to give to the care and cultivation of friendship the attention it needs. Too often people who would go to endless pains to save a marriage or to patch up a decaying relationship with a child or parent will, like Woodrow Wilson, let a friendship go to ruin over a single quarrel or misunderstanding. There is no commandment in the Decalogue to honor a friend. And at our funerals and weddings the most distant cousin is given a better pew than the closest and dearest friend.

Perhaps, however, one of the values of friendship is precisely that it is not defined or classified or put in any kind of an ordinary cubbyhole. Friends do not have to be supported, like wives and minor children; they are not heirs, and their elimination requires no divorce. Our moral obligations to our friends are like gambling debts, legally unenforceable. Communion between us is free and voluntary. If friendship lacks the wings of love, it is also spared the pangs. Its spirit is so beautifully caught in William Cory's poem "Heraclitus" that, famous as it is, I presume to quote it again.

They told me, Heraclitus, they told me you were dead;
They brought me bitter news to hear and bitter tears to
      shed.
I wept as I remembered how often you and I
Had tired the sun with talking and sent him down the
      sky.

And now that thou art lying, my dear old Carian guest,
A handful of grey ashes, long, long ago at rest,
Still are thy pleasant voices, thy Nightingales, awake,
For Death, he taketh all away, but them he cannot take.

Woodrow Wilson

and

Colonel House

$\mathcal{T}$HERE IS certainly no more important friendship in American political history than that of Woodrow Wilson and Edward M. House (always known as Colonel House, the title in the Texas militia conferred upon him by Governor James S. Hogg, whose campaigns he had managed), but I question whether the term "friendship" precisely defines their relationship.

To Wilson's mind their seven year intimacy, born of a single meeting, bordered on the mystical. They met on November 24, 1911, at the Gotham Hotel in New York City. House was already well known for his brilliant campaign work for the Democratic Party in Texas, and now that the fell influence of William Jennings Bryan, who had so long and so disastrously dominated the party, was at last on the wane, he was searching for a candidate who might defeat Taft in 1912. He and Wilson seemed to understand each other at once, and the latter wrote to him, "My dear friend, we have known each other always."

With a solidly united Texas delegation at the convention in

Baltimore, and with Bryan by a miracle of diplomacy brought into the Wilson camp, House was given wide credit for the victory of his candidate over Taft and Roosevelt; and Wilson, as President, told a politician in 1913: "Mr. House is my second personality. He is my independent self. If I were in his place, I would do just as he suggested. If anyone thinks he is reflecting my opinion by whatever action he takes, they are welcome to the conclusion."

And he acknowledged House's congratulations on the passage of legislation he had sponsored in even stronger terms:

> Your letter on the passage of the Tariff Bill gave me the kind of pleasure that seldom comes to a man, and it goes so deep that no words are adequate to express it. I think you must know without my putting it into words (for I cannot) how deep such friendship and support goes with me and how large a part it constitutes of such strength as I have in public affairs. I thank you with all my heart and with deep affection.

Wilson, despite an exterior that struck some who met him as at least formal, at times cold and perhaps on occasion even arrogant, was a deeply emotional man. He was intensely and dependently in love with each of his wives, and the warmth of his correspondence with a woman friend, if published, threatened to arouse grave misunderstanding. He enjoyed reading poetry aloud to his dinner guests and engaging with his few intimates in long discussions of literature, ethics and the immortality of the soul.

House was very much his opposite, even physically. Whereas Wilson was tall and handsome, impressive as a statesman and orator, House was short and frail (he had been afflicted by malaria as a youth), with a receding chin and a voice that lacked resonance. Recognizing early that he was not endowed for the political arena, he had adopted the role of advisor behind the scenes. His nature was drier and more practical than Wilson's, and although there is little doubt that he was devoted to the President, his essential interest was in how he could use and manipulate him. Use and manipulate him for a great goal, I concede — nothing short of world concord — but is this friendship in the deepest sense? Let us call it, anyway, a kind of friendship. House's diary shows that he was constantly studying Wilson, adapting himself carefully to the latter's changing moods, lavishly praising him (adverse criticism — and it was frequent — being confined to private pages) and ever alert to catch the right moment for the suggestion of a plan. House believed in all sincerity that Wilson was the hope of the civilized world, but that hope would be realized only by a Wilson directed and moderated by House.

There had to be conceit in such a notion, but the reader of the four volumes of *The Intimate Papers of Colonel House,* edited by Charles Seymour and published from 1926 to 1928, will find himself intrigued by the possibility that there may have been some truth in it. He must also bear in mind, however, the caveat of Walter Lippmann: "Just exactly what Colonel House did no one will ever know for certain." For almost all that he did was in private talks with the President and a small circle of influential men and is "indistinguishably fused with Woodrow Wilson."

Lippmann, who had worked closely with House in drafting the Fourteen Points to be presented to the Peace Conference that was to follow the war, wrote a column on the Colonel's death in 1938, which brilliantly summarized House's value to Wilson. Wilson, according to Lippmann, was an intellectual, accustomed to acquiring knowledge by reading and to imparting it by giving lectures and writing books, whereas House learned what he had to know and communicated it almost solely by word of mouth, dealing with men face to face.

Thus Colonel House brought to Wilson a faculty which Wilson lacked, though it is essential to a statesman. No one can be President of the United States without having a great variety of personal contacts. And Wilson did not like personal contact, and instinctively shrank from it . . . Through Colonel House he remained in communication with men from whom he would otherwise have been shut away. For the Colonel, lacking Wilson's fierce convictions about ideas, had ever so much easier and broader sympathies with ordinary human beings. From this there came, so it always seemed to me, the thing which saved Wilson's administration from the fanatical and sectarian narrowness that is so often the undoing of reformers.

House may have lacked Wilson's "fierce convictions," but only in the sense that he never forgot that compromise was often essential to their implementation. A dream unrealized is only a dream. It is important, however, in understanding House to recognize that he had his dream and never lost it, and that he had it long before Wilson had the same. It was the vision of world peace.

The desperate lawlessness that surrounded his father's great plantation in Fort Bend County, Texas, made a deep and lasting impression on House as a boy. He later recalled two young men of the neighborhood, roommates, who killed each other in a gun duel at ten paces because one had put his muddy boots on the bed they occupied in common. "I can hardly realize," he wrote, "that so short a while ago we lived in an atmosphere where such things seemed proper and even a matter of course. I was often with men who I knew would surely be killed soon and perhaps at a time when I was with them . . . People praised us Southerners for our courteous demeanor; we learned it in a school of necessity."

Despite Lippmann's contention that House was fundamentally a man of oral communication, he did write and publish, anonymously, in 1912, a novel, *Philip Dru, Administrator*. It is a very bad novel; indeed it is hardly a novel at all, but rather a fabric of pasteboard characters mouthing political principles, which ends with the text of a new American Constitution drafted by the eponymous hero. But it is of some interest that the hero sees the need of a league of nations and is willing to use force to achieve his goal. House was always readier than Wilson to have the United States join the Allies in the war, because he believed that an Allied victory offered the only hope for lasting peace.

When Wilson took office in 1913, House embarked on a full-time job as presidential advisor. He did not, however, accept any official position or emolument, or even move to Washington. He may have seen that his influence would be greater if his presence were less noted. He remained in his apartment in New York and continued to pass his summers on the Massachusetts shore; his dread of heat kept him from the simmering capital in even the worst crises. When he went to Washington he stayed at the White House, and when Wilson came to New York he stayed with the Houses, even sharing a bathroom with his host.

The choice of the private role was entirely House's; Wilson offered him any position in the Cabinet he wanted except State, which both men agreed had to go to Bryan. But House argued to himself that should he be in the Cabinet and his advice on a particular issue not be taken, he would have the disagreeable alternatives of resigning or enforcing a policy of which he did not approve. As a private individual he could simply turn his attention to other matters where he might prove more successful in convincing the President to act.

But his role in the administration was not by any means confined to advice. He talked to people whom the President didn't want to see and even acted for him in announcing appointments. Walter Hines Page learned that he had been named ambassador to the United Kingdom from House's cheerful greeting on the telephone: "Good morning, Your Excellency!" And David Houston was not even sure that he should go to Washington. He told Page, "I have never to this good day received any notification of my appointment as Secretary of Agriculture excepting that which I received from Colonel House."

In 1915 Wilson sent House on a mission to the capitals of the belligerent powers to explore the possibilities of a negotiated peace. House was surprised, dining at the White House on the eve of his departure, to find that the President preferred reading aloud to discussing business. "He evidently had confidence in my doing the work I came to Washington for, without his help."

He did, however, accompany House to the station the next day: "The President's eyes were moist when he said his last words of farewell." House then entered in his diary his most explicit account of what his relationship with Wilson meant to him. It is a moving statement, but it has more to do with House than with Wilson, more with his life goal than with friendship:

> I asked if he remembered the first day we met, some three and a half years ago. He replied, "Yes, but we had known one another always, and merely came in touch then, for our purposes and thoughts were as one." I told him how much he had been to me; how I had tried all my life to find someone with whom I could work out the things I had so deeply at heart, and I had begun to despair, believing my life should be more or less a failure, when he came into it, giving me the opportunity for which I had been longing.

On this trip and on his second in 1916 House battled in vain against the intransigency of the war leaders on both sides.

England could not be induced to limit her blockade, nor could Germany be persuaded to restrict her submarine warfare. Germany would never consent to pay reparations to Belgium, nor France to mitigate in the least her claims for all of Alsace-Lorraine. Both sides were locked in a seemingly permanent and suicidal conflict, each determined to achieve total victory at any price. House wrote in discouragement to Wilson from Paris in February of 1916:

> In each government I have visited I have found stubbornness, determination, selfishness, and cant. One continually hears self-glorification and the highest motives attributed to themselves because of their part in the war. But I may tell you that my observation is that incompetent statesmanship and selfishness is at the bottom of it all. It is not so much a breaking down of civilization as a lack of wisdom in those that govern; and history, I believe, will bring an awful indictment against those who were short-sighted and selfish enough to let such a tragedy happen.

House was immune to the growing and passionate faith among the Allies and many Americans that the war was a crusade against Satan. He was disgusted with Cecil Spring-Rice, the British ambassador in Washington, who believed, almost hysterically, that House should have no dealings with the German envoy, and he regarded Walter Hines Page more as an officer of the British crown than an American diplomat. But he perfectly understood the force of their feeling, and he tried in vain to keep Wilson from stating in public what both privately believed, that "the causes and objects of the war are obscure." But Wilson was obdurate and put the offending sentence in a public appeal for a negotiated peace. House noted bitterly: "He seems obsessed with that thought and he cannot write or talk on the subject of the war without voicing it. It has done more to make him unpopular in the Allied countries than any one thing he has done, and it will probably keep him from taking the part which he ought to take in peace negotiations . . . It is all so unnecessary. He could have done and said the same things in a different way."

House at this time was also deeply upset by Wilson's failure to inaugurate a giant preparedness program. "I am convinced that the President's place in history is dependent to a large degree on luck. If we should get into a serious war and it should turn out disastrously he would be one of the most discredited presidents we have had . . . We have no large guns."

Indeed, considering the outward attitude of consistent admiration, of almost hero worship, that House maintained towards the President, his private conclusions about Wilson's failings are sufficiently startling. One must remember that they are without spite; it was his simple duty, as he probably saw it, to be constantly assessing the assets and liabilities of the man who was to save the world. Here are a few:

"He dodges trouble. Let me put something up to him that is disagreeable, and I have great difficulty getting him to meet it."

"Another phase of his character is the intensity of his prejudices against people. He likes a few and is very loyal to them, but his prejudices are many and often unjust. He finds great difficulty in conferring with men against whom, for some reason, he has a prejudice and in whom he can find nothing good."

"I am afraid that the President's characterization of himself as 'a man with a one-track mind' is all too true, for he does not seem able to carry along more than one idea at a time."

"The President, as I have often said before, is too casual and does the most important things sometimes without much reflection."

When Germany's now totally unrestricted submarine attacks on neutral vessels drove America at last to war, House did all he could to buck up his chief in a moment of understandable depression. The crisis drove him from his usual caution and flattery, and for once he spoke out boldly:

> I told him a crisis had come in his administration different from anything he had yet encountered, and I was anxious that he should meet it in a creditable way so that his influence would not be lessened when he came to do the great work which would necessarily follow the war. I said it was not as difficult a situation as many he had already successfully met, but that it was one for which he was not well fitted. He admitted this and said he did not believe he was fitted for the presidency under such conditions. I thought he was too refined, too civilized, too intellectual, too cultivated not to see the incongruity and absurdity of war. It needs a man of coarser fibre, and one less a philosopher than the President, to conduct a brutal, vigorous, and successful war.

This might seem hardly the kind of fight talk a beleaguered chief of state needed, but House knew his man, if the following entry is to be credited:

> I made him feel, as Mrs. Wilson told me later, that he was not up against so difficult a proposition as he had imagined. In my argument I said that everything that he had to meet in this emergency had been thought out time and time again in other countries, and all we had to do was to take experience as our guide and not worry over the manner of doing it.

If Mrs. Wilson really approved of House's bizarre method of bracing her husband's morale, it must have been effective, for she was the Colonel's most implacable enemy.

Wilson, at any rate, turned out to be a far more vigorous

and successful war President than many people, including himself, had anticipated, and the two men seem to have worked together happily during the conflict. House was for much of the time with the War Mission in London, but in January of 1918 he was back in Washington, working on the draft of the Fourteen Points to be presented to the ultimate Peace Conference. We catch this glimpse of him working with Wilson on the final version:

> Saturday was a remarkable day. I went over to the State Department just after breakfast to see Polk [Frank L. Polk, Under Secretary of State] and others, and returned to the White House at a quarter past ten in order to get to work with the President. He was waiting for me. We actually got down to work at half-past ten and finished remaking the map of the world, as we would have it, at half-past twelve o'clock.

Wilson appointed a Peace Commission of five, headed by himself, to represent the United States at the Versailles Conference. Secretary of State Robert Lansing was an obvious choice, and General Tasker Bliss was the necessary military man. A fourth member, Henry White, an able diplomat and former ambassador to France and Italy, had all the credentials so far as talent and experience were concerned, but as the one Republican on the team his selection was almost an insult to the majority party in a Senate that would have to ratify any treaty entered into. For White had never been even a candidate for elected office; his party affiliation was simply as a registered voter and (he was a wealthy man) no doubt a contributor. And a fifth member, House himself, was an even worse choice.

He had explained in 1913, when he refused any post in the Cabinet, that if he had taken one he would have been less free to advise the President in appointing the others. This must have been just as true of the Peace Commission. A man who had made a career of political astuteness could not have been unaware of the glaring error of the White appointment. In later years House admitted that Wilson had been politically inexpedient in this respect and that William Howard Taft or Elihu Root would have been a better choice. But he always insisted on the undeniably high calibre of the commission as composed by the President, and it is hard not to suppose that the latter's naming of House not only mitigated the latter's criticism of Wilson's cavalier treatment of the opposing political party but blinded him to the fact that he was throwing away his own ace of trumps. For what was that but the unique influence that his hitherto rigidly preserved independence had given him in the mind and heart of Woodrow Wilson?

House had now taken a post where he would have to work *with* the President. He would no longer be able to stand aside and offer calm and sound advice when asked for it. He would very likely have to oppose the President, and in matters, too, that were of the deepest concern to Wilson. How could this not appear as a kind of betrayal to a man of impatient and authoritarian temperament from one who had hitherto offered him nothing but the most gratifying support?

Yet one can see why House allowed himself to be tempted. Here at long last was the supreme opportunity to realize the dream of a lifetime, of achieving world concord. Why should he care, if *that* was achieved, what happened to his friendship with Wilson? Was he not more equipped for the job than the President? Did he not know personally and almost intimately many of the highest representatives of the Allied powers? Had he not traveled over Europe to discuss terms of peace with their chiefs of state? And everyone knew that diplomacy was not Wilson's forte; he was too uncompromising, too idealistic, too irritable. Let him stay home until the work, including the dirty work that such a conference would necessarily entail, was done.

But Wilson had no idea of staying home, and when House, who had preceded him to Paris, cabled to him that the feeling of the delegates was distinctly against his coming, he replied with a chilly note which should have warned House that things were already changing between them. Wilson suggested sternly that House was too much under the influence of the British and French leaders, and voiced this warning: "I hope you will be very shy of their advice and give me your own independent judgment after reconsideration."

Independent judgment! What was that but the Colonel's principal asset? Wilson was afraid he had already lost it.

The President came to Paris, and his first visit lasted until February 14, 1919, when the Covenant of the League of Nations was agreed upon. It was the last good moment between him and the Colonel. After Wilson's speech, House passed him a penciled note of hearty congratulation, which Wilson passed back to him with the annotation: "Bless your heart. Thank you from the bottom of my heart."

The seed of suspicion had been planted, but it had not yet sprouted. The President, fearing that Secretary Lansing had become lukewarm about the League, considered asking for his resignation so that House could be head of the American Peace Commission during Wilson's planned absence of a month in Washington. But House, according to Mrs. Wilson, persuaded her husband not to rock the boat. It would be enough to leave the titular supremacy with Lansing and the real authority in House's competent hands.

Edith Bolling Wilson had never liked House since the time when he had unsuccessfully urged Wilson to postpone his marriage to her at least until the second presidential campaign was over. And she had never got over the abrupt way she had seen him change his position on the government's taking over the railroads in wartime the moment he had seen the President firmly favor the step. She felt there was no depth or sincerity in her husband's advisor. When she and Wilson returned to France on March 14, the Colonel met them at Brest, and he and the President were closeted for an hour in the latter's private railway car. Wilson emerging, she related in *My Memoir,* looked ten years older.

"House has given away everything I had wrought before we left Paris," he told her bleakly. "He has compromised on every side, and so I have to start all over again."

Edith obviously believed that House had betrayed her husband by working furiously in his absence to make the compromises he knew his idealistic chief would never make and so present him with a *fait accompli* on his return. But the concessions made to the vengeful Allies, who insisted on the occupation of the Saar Valley and the Rhine and who wanted to cripple Germany with impossible reparations, were ultimately agreed to by Wilson himself. He may have been debilitated by the flu, which he contracted shortly after his second arrival in Paris, or he may have simply come to believe that the British and French leaders were hopelessly obdurate, but both he and House seem to have agreed that the League was the only thing that could be extracted from the mess. To some extent they may have justified Senator Henry Cabot Lodge's later claim that Wilson had traded a treaty that everyone despised for a league that nobody wanted.

Edith Wilson now became relentless in her efforts to make her husband see what she considered the light about his supposed friend. But there was still a fund of resistance in Wilson. When she called House a "perfect jellyfish," he replied, "Well, God made jellyfish, so, as Shakespeare said about a man, therefore let him pass, and don't be too hard on House." And when she went further and charged House with leaking stories to the press through his son-in-law, Gordon Auchincloss, to the effect that he and not Wilson was the real brains of the American commission, Wilson protested that he would as soon doubt her own loyalty as House's. But one cannot but suspect that it was here that she began to make her point, and I imagine that House knew this when he went to the station to bid what turned out to be a last farewell to his chief. "My last conversation with the President was not reassuring. I urged him to meet the Senate in a conciliatory spirit; if he treated them with the same consideration he had used with his foreign colleagues here, all would be well. In reply he said: 'House, I have found one can never get anything in this life that is worthwhile without fighting for it.' "

Wilson would have no more to do, it was clear, with his former friend's diplomatic way of handling the enemies of world peace. In his present mood the long, anguished and ultimately unsuccessful fight for the ratification of the treaty was probably foreseen by the perspicacious Colonel. House may have also understood that his own life work was doomed.

There did not have to be a formal break. Four days before the President left on his tour of the nation to gather public support for the treaty, he cabled House, who was still in Paris, "Am deeply distressed by malicious story about break between us . . . The best way to treat it is with silent contempt."

In October both men fell ill, Wilson with a stroke. House got no call to come to Washington, but he received three short notes in response to his own, signed "Faithfully yours" or "Sincerely yours," but not "Affectionately." They did not meet again.

House wrote to Charles Seymour, the editor of his *Intimate Papers,* on April 20, 1928:

There were many doors in the temples that men of old reared to their gods, to the sun, to the moon, to the mythical deities, Isis, Jupiter, Mars. Behind the innermost door dwelt the mysteries. And now you, who have had access to my most intimate papers, ask me to unlock the innermost door, a door to which I have no key. My separation from Woodrow Wilson was and is to me a tragic mystery, a mystery that now can never be dispelled, for its explanation lies buried with him. Theories I have, and theories they must remain. These you know.

Never, during the years we worked together, was there an unkind or impatient word, written or spoken, and this, to me, is an abiding consolation.

While our friendship was not of long duration it was as close as human friendships grow to be. To this his letters and mine bear silent testimony. Until a shadow fell between us I never had a more considerate friend, and my devotion to his memory remains and will remain unchanged.

The publication of *The Intimate Papers* created a furor of indignation that has not entirely died down to this day. Mrs. Wilson and her husband's physician, Admiral Clay T. Grayson, took particular umbrage, claiming, with some justification, that the Colonel had represented himself as the late President's genius, as something even more than a grey eminence, almost indeed a puppeteer pulling the strings of his marionette. House, perhaps unintentionally, had certainly created a disproportionate picture of his influence on Wilson. The latter's intellect and personality were notoriously too forceful to have been as subject to House's persuasion as *The Intimate Papers* seem to imply. And I cannot get away from my own impression that the Colonel's intellect was more dry and factual than brilliant, more analytical than imaginative, and that his observations tended to be rather tediously laden with truisms and clichés. I believe that Walter Lippmann was correct in supposing that his greatest value to Wilson was in talking to people with whom Wilson did not wish to talk, and it is obvious that in their personal relations the President preferred reading aloud to his friend to listening to him.

On January 3, 1938, less than three months before the Colonel's death at age seventy-nine, he agreed at last to talk to Charles Seymour about the cause of his separation from Wilson, provided that Seymour would not reveal it until twenty-five years after his demise. And in 1963 Seymour did so, in an article in *American Heritage* magazine.

As many had long suspected, the cause was Mrs. Wilson. "I am told by those who were in Washington," House had asserted to Seymour, "that Mrs. Wilson was determined to come to the Peace Conference. I have also been told that she made plain that she thought I was trying to steal the President's thunder abroad and pose as the director of American foreign policy." House had gone on to say that Mrs. Wilson in Paris had resented the praise accorded to the Colonel by the press and had excluded him from the President's intimate circle. By the time the Peace Conference closed, Bernard Baruch, who was now constantly with the Wilsons, indicated to House that he had taken his place as the President's confidant. After the Wilsons returned to Washington, House suspected that Mrs. Wilson deliberately kept her now-invalid husband in ignorance of House's letters and barred his visits to the sickbed. In the end she even excluded him from Wilson's funeral.

And now let me suppose that House had refused a seat on the Peace Commission. Suppose he had confined himself to his old role of proferring advice only when asked, might he not have retained Wilson's total confidence and been in a position to steer him through the struggle with Lodge and his cohorts in the Senate? Might Wilson, weary and ill, not even have left in his hands some of the negotiations about the Lodge reservations to the treaty? And had the United States joined the League, surely some of the injustices of the treaty could have been earlier mitigated.

The little Colonel, anyway, was appreciated by one important war leader. Eugenia B. Frothingham described for the *Boston Transcript* on February 25, 1928, her interview with former Prime Minister Asquith shortly before his death:

> I asked him if the statesmen of Europe struggling for breath and life during the World War did not ultimately tire of Colonel House and his various peace plans, and ask themselves why this small unofficial person should keep thrusting himself into their affairs. At this Asquith struck the terrace with his cane and said there would have been more of breath and life if the plans of Colonel House had been acted upon.

In June of 1914, just before the outbreak of Armageddon, House had toured the capitals of the about-to-be-belligerent powers in a last-ditch effort to preserve the peace. He was received by the Kaiser in Potsdam at the Schrippenfest, or White Roll Feast, which he described as a "gorgeous presentation of devotional militarism in the Prussian style, such as the Kaiser loved dearly." House, a rare civilian in that glittering array, a sober small figure in black, talked at some length and to little purpose with the splendidly pompous and empty-headed monarch. I doubt that he was more impressed with him than he had been, so many years before, by the two misguided youths in Fort Bend County who had blown each other's brains out at ten paces.

JUSTICE HOLMES

and

SIR FREDERICK POLLOCK

*An Epistolary
Friendship*

$\mathcal{O}$LIVER WENDELL HOLMES, JR., was born in 1841 and died ninety-four years later. His almost lifelong friend, Sir Frederick Pollock, third baronet, was born four years after him and survived him by two. Their correspondence, beginning in 1874 and continuing for sixty-one years, embraces almost every aspect of the high but increasingly threatened civilization that had produced this finely civilized pair.

Holmes was of old Boston stock, the son of the famous doctor and essayist for whom he was named, but not rich. The law was the love of his life, but it had also to be his support; he practiced it until he was forty and served thereafter as a judge, first on the Massachusetts and then on the United States Supreme Court, for the rest of his long life. He had time to produce only one book, a classic, *The Common Law,* and an edition of *Kent's Commentaries.* Pollock, on the other hand, was a rich man, of a distinguished judicial family, who had time for the prodigious scholarship in the common law that produced, among many learned works, *Principles of Contract*

(1876), *The Law of Torts* (1887) and, in collaboration with Frederic W. Maitland, the great *History of English Law before the Time of Edward I* (1895). The shared passion of the two men for the history and development of law at first motivated and for a while dominated their correspondence, but with time the tenor of their letters broadened to embrace all matters suggested by their omnivorous and eclectic reading.

What makes these letters uniquely interesting is the quality of the friendship and the character of the writers. Many of Holmes's ideas are equally well expressed in his correspondence with Harold Laski. But there the reader is confronted simply with the exchange of thoughts. Holmes was much more interested in Laski the thinker than he was in Laski the man, whose hyperactive imagination bordered at times on a seemingly compulsive mendacity. But in the correspondence with Pollock the reader is always dealing with a meeting of the hearts as well as the minds, with an interchange of ideas and affections between two persons who are "men" in the stongest and best sense of that word, and who are also "gentlemen," in the finest meaning of a term that is today often considered pejorative.

Indeed, it is a tricky business to describe the sterling qualities of Holmes and Pollock without seeming snobbish or elitist. But the risk must be taken, for I believe we should never lose sight of the concept of sturdy, of even ruthless independence from popular opinion, popular politics, popular morality and popular religion that these two men represent.

Perhaps Wendell Holmes, of the two, carried his independence of mind and action the furthest. He fought through three years of combat in the Civil War and was three times severely wounded, yet at the end of his term of enlistment, and with the last eight (and, as it turned out, bloodiest) months of the war still to be fought, he resigned his commission to enter as a law student at Harvard. In coming to his decision, he considered nobody's opinion but his own. Here is what he wrote to his parents:

> I started this thing as a boy. I am now a man and I have been coming to the conclusion for the last six months that my duty has changed. I can do a disagreeable thing or face a danger coolly enough when I *know* it is a duty — but a doubt demoralizes me as it does any nervous man — and I honestly think the duty of fighting has ceased for me — ceased because I have laboriously and with much suffering of mind and body *earned* the right . . . to decide for myself how I can best do my duty to myself, to the country, and, if you choose, to God.

As an old man Holmes came to question the validity of this decision. But it was certainly consistent with his concept of independence. He never shrank before the enemy, nor did he shrink before the prospect of what his family and friends might think of his packing up and going home before Richmond had been taken. Certainly he never regarded this decision as qualifying his right to extol the military virtues to youth.

Indeed, he did the latter to a degree that may be offensive to modern ears. He never lost sight of the innate brutality of man, and he believed that converting it into the grace of the warrior was the noblest use it could be put to. As he said in a Memorial Day address at Harvard in 1895:

> War, when you are at it, is horrible and dull. It is only when time has passed that you see that its message was divine . . . for high and dangerous action teaches us to believe as right beyond dispute things for which our doubting minds are slow to find words of proof. Out of heroism grows faith in the worth of heroism. The proof comes later, and even may never come. Therefore I rejoice at every dangerous sport which I see pursued. The students at Heidelberg, with their sword-slashed faces, inspire me with sincere respect. I gaze with delight upon our polo players. If once in a while in our rough riding a neck

is broken, I regard it, not as a waste, but as a price well paid for the breeding of a race fit for headship and command.

Yet not for Holmes was the blustering masculinity of Theodore Roosevelt, and when the latter, who had appointed him to the Supreme Court, exhibited a lively indignation that he should dare vote against the government's antitrust position in the *Northern Securities* case, Holmes simply shrugged. Referring to the incident years later, on TR's death, he wrote to Pollock:

> We [he and the President] talked freely later, but it never was the same after that, and if he had not been restrained by his friends, I am told he would have made a fool of himself and would have excluded me from the White House. I never cared a damn whether I went there or not. He was very likeable, a big figure, a rather ordinary intellect, with extraordinary gifts, a shrewd and I think pretty unscrupulous politician. He played all his cards — if not more. R.I.P.

Holmes enjoyed a great reputation as a liberal, but this meant nothing to him. His only interest was in the good opinion of such peers as Pollock, and never in the praise or dispraise of "a lot of duffers, generally I think not even lawyers, talking with the sanctity of print in a way that at once discloses to the knowing eye that literally they don't know anything about it." He wrote to Pollock in 1890 that some respectable persons were beginning to regard him as a dangerous radical. "If I had seen fit to clothe my views in different language I daresay I could have been a pet of the proletariat — whereas they care nothing for me."

His belief that the government elected by the majority should be allowed a wide range in socially remedial legislation did not at all reflect his own approval of it. He was simply so skeptical about "the goodness or badness of laws" that he had "no practical criticism except what the crowd wants." Nor did he believe in soaking the rich, in "hate and envy for those who have any luxury, as wrongdoers." He regarded the railway magnate James J. Hill as "representing one of the greatest forms of human power, an immense mastery of economic details, an equal grasp of general principles, an ability and courage to put his conclusions into practice with brilliant success where all the knowing ones said he would fail." The vast fortunes of such men he considered a drop in the bucket, the division of which among the multitude would not improve their well-being. "I think the crowd now has substantially all there is."

And where freedom of speech was concerned, no champion can have ever less valued the words he was called upon to protect. For it was not, after all, the opinions of Aristotle or Emerson whose expression the Court was usually asked to guard. What was more often threatened was the shrieks of anarchists and religious fanatics, involving the right, as Holmes succinctly put it, of "a fool to drool."

Sir Frederick Pollock never had to serve in a war, but he was a devoted fencer and a passionate mountain climber in Switzerland. He met Holmes when the latter visited England in the summer of 1874, and, as he expressed it, "there was no stage of acquaintance ripening into friendship; we understood one another and were friends without more ado." One can understand the immediate attraction between the two. Mark De Wolfe Howe, editor of their correspondence, wrote of Pollock: "He was vigorous and direct. If a certain brusqueness veiled a suggestion of shyness which made his casual conversation sometimes hesitating, there was nothing halting about his pungent and sometimes caustic conclusions and expressions and his prepared addresses."

Pollock early gave up the practice of law for teaching and scholarship. He was a professor of law at the Inns of Court and at Oxford, and for forty years held down the exhausting and meticulous job of editor-in-chief of the Law Reports. He and Holmes were in early agreement that the life of the law was experience rather than logic; that it might be defined as a statement of the circumstances in which the public force would be brought to bear upon a man by the courts, and never as a divine code, snatched, so to speak, from on high. They were realists in law and in philosophy, skeptics who were all the more eager to make something noble and beautiful out of the present, should the present turn out to be all there was.

"On the whole I am on the side of the unregenerate who affirm the worth of life as an end in itself as against the saints who deny it," Holmes wrote to Lady Pollock in 1902. "I may whisper in your ear that the male saints whom I have seen near to have been flats."

In the early years the correspondence dealt largely with law. Holmes, working at night on the essays that would make up *The Common Law,* his days more than taken up by his law practice, was completely absorbed by his theory that law, both criminal and civil, had no concern with a man's subjective intent, but only with what a "reasonable" man should have intended under the given circumstances. Pollock was in accord, but one sometimes gets the impression that he found Holmes riding his hobbyhorse a bit too hard. "I quite agree with you that legal negligence is not a state of mind," he wrote in 1880. Such negligence, he conceded, was simply the falling short of an objective standard of conduct. But then he added, "The thought of man is not triable, for the devil himself knows not the thought of man."

.   .   .

But by 1887 the correspondence had moved to a more personal plane, and we find Holmes, like his friend Henry James's hero Lambert Strether, in *The Ambassadors,* emphasizing the vital importance of living such life as one is fortunate enough to have: "But I am very happy and I always think that when a man has once had his chance — has reached the tableland above his difficulties — it does not matter so much whether he has more or less time allowed him in that stage. The real anguish is never to have your opportunity. I used to think of that a good deal during the war."

And later we find him writing to Lady Pollock: "You may say what you like about American women — and I won't be unpatriotic — but English women are brought up, it seems to me, to realize that it is an object to be charming, that man is a dangerous animal — or ought to be — and that a sexless *bonhomie* is not the ideal relation."

The Pollocks were a more sophisticated pair than the Holmeses. Sir Frederick, enjoying the Victorian upper-class assumption that life in each new deal was apt to hand you a few trump cards, rarely struck (although he was a poet as well as a legal scholar) Holmes's emotional note, and his wife was obviously more lively than the sweet but neurotic Fannie Holmes, who preferred working by the fireside on her beautiful embroideries to accompanying her brilliant husband into a society where she could not emulate his wit.

Holmes even wrote to his friend on the bench during oral arguments:

As we don't shut up bores one has to listen to discourses dragging slowly along after one has seen the point and made up one's mind. That is what is happening now and I take the chance to write as I sit with my brethren. I hope I shall be supposed to be taking notes.

"Goodbye, dear lad, I am a little blue," he ended one letter to Pollock. "I don't quite know why and feel older." Pollock was less intimate in describing his feelings, but he wrote: "Your outlook on things in general is much after my own heart." And when, in 1909, he had "fevered dreams" in a bout with influenza, he tried to describe one of them to Holmes. But one is not surprised that Pollock's dream was something less than feverish. He received a "revelation" that the appointed seat for a future grand court for the English-speaking nations would be the Scilly Islands — for the ease of excluding reporters!

The two friends were constantly exchanging views in philosophy. Pollock wrote in 1919:

> It is long since I have looked at any general history of philosophy. Talk about man's cosmic importance has very little meaning for me. From the exterior or natural history point of view — the sensible universe as a continuous orderly whole — one phenomenon is as important as another. From the interior point of view of man as a living soul we know nothing of his importance among the infinite possible orders of intelligence in the spiritual world, assuming them to be commensurable — which may be a large assumption.

To which Holmes replied: "Some want a universal world to hold the world together, others do not. For myself I find it difficult to believe that the universe is reasonable, but impossible to believe that it is not."

In 1920, after the world conflict in which both men were far too old to have any active part, Holmes wrote:

> I loathe war — which I described when at home with a wound in our Civil War as an organized bore — to the scandal of the young women of the day who thought that Captain Holmes

was wanting in patriotism. But I do think that man at present is a predatory animal. I think that the sacredness of human life is a purely municipal ideal of no validity outside the jurisdiction. I believe that force, mitigated so far as may be by good manners, is the *ultima ratio,* and between two groups that want to make inconsistent kinds of world I see no remedy except force. I may add what I no doubt have said often enough, that it seems to me that every society rests on the death of men — as does also the romantic interest of long-inhabited lands.

Pollock replied:

As to the sanctity of human life I quite agree with you that there is too much fuss about it. My complaint against war is not that it kills men but that it kills the wrong ones, taking an undue proportion of the strong and adventurous and leaving too many weaklings and shirkers, thus working a perverse artificial selection of those who are least fitted to adorn or improve the commonwealth.

And he added, in a subsequent letter, what to him must have been a rare acknowledgment of deep feeling:

Which reminds me how I might have reinforced my doctrine as to the contra-natural selection of war by the example of a certain stray bullet whose deviation by a fraction of an inch would have deprived the learned world of *The Common Law,* the law itself of the judgement aforesaid [referring to a recent Holmes opinion] and many other profitable ones, the dissenting ones not the least so, and the present writer of a friendship nearing its jubilee, one of some three or four that have counted most in his life.

In the 1920s and 1930s the two friends kept up-to-date with all the better books that were coming out and exchanged one-sentence reviews. It is disappointing but hardly surprising that neither much cared for Proust. Pollock felt that "life was too short to do more than dip into" him, and Holmes thought he took an unconscionable time over things and people "that he doesn't make me much care for." But then Holmes felt that Henry James had showed "a touch of underbreeding in his recurrence to the problem of the social relations of Americans to the old world." It was also predictable that Holmes should have preferred "fresh and agreeable and even noble people" to Ernest Hemingway's "sordid situations and bad smells." But one is glad that both he and Pollock were enchanted with *Gentlemen Prefer Blondes* and that Holmes was "unexpectedly and deeply moved" by *My Ántonia.* And in any consideration of literature in respect to these correspondents it must always be remembered that George Meredith dedicated *Diana of the Crossways* to Pollock in 1885.

In 1931 Holmes wrote to his friend of the latter's laudatory piece in the Columbia Law Review on the Justice's ninetieth birthday: "It would put heart into a brass andiron, and I shall die the happier for it."

Holmes had occasion to congratulate his friend on another sort of accomplishment. Pollock was not yet quite ninety, but he took on two ruffians who waylaid him on the empty stairway of a public building in London and routed them by jabbing his umbrella right in their eyes. The long years of fencing paid off, and the Civil War veteran was proud of his embattled junior.

$\mathcal{B}$OSWELL

and

$\mathcal{J}$OHNSON

$\mathcal{T}$HE 1937 DISCOVERY at Malahide Castle in Ireland of the great box of his journals and other papers revealed a James Boswell vastly more interesting and complicated than the man previously conceived. Here was a person of prodigious industry, of moods varying from the dizzily elated to the abysmally low, an acute and astute observer of every detail of things going on around him, a cultivator of the friendship of more great men than the one with whom his name had been almost exclusively associated, an earnestly would-be-faithful husband and an inveterate womanizer. It was not only now evident that he was a writer of genius, who had hitherto been esteemed only a reporter of that quality; it was also understandable why Samuel Johnson could write to him, "I have heard you mentioned as a man whom everybody likes." He was, in Johnson's term, innately "clubable."

Before then it had been something of a fashion to sneer at Boswell and to regard his *Life of Johnson* as one of the inexplicable wonders of the British eighteenth century. Cyril Connolly deemed him "silly, snobbish, lecherous, given to high-flown sentiments and more than a little of a humbug." Lytton Strachey found him "an idler, a lecher, a drunkard and a snob."

I don't suppose that in our day it is necessary to deal with the charges of lechery (from Strachey!) and drunkenness, both of which are regarded as simple weaknesses, and even by some as amiable ones, but nobody could regard the author of the Malahide archives as an idler, and Boswell was a snob only in the sense that he had a great regard for his noble ancestry and for the prerogatives of rank, a common enough trait in the upper class of his day. Indeed, Wilmarth Lewis, who devoted a long life to the study of the century, states in his biography of Horace Walpole that the word "snob" had not yet been invented in either of its senses, that is, the looking up to or down from a position of superior rank or wealth, and that "to call Walpole a snob for regarding Gray and Ashton as his social inferiors is to impose upon the eighteenth century an epithet that it would not have understood."

"Silly" may be fair. Boswell was certainly that at times, though how many of us would not show that aspect of our nature if we revealed as much of ourselves as he did? "Naïve" might be a more accurate and less pejorative term. Connolly's "high-flown sentiments" I consider an integral part of Boswell's literary style and his "humbug" merely a term of abuse.

But perhaps the greatest revelation of the Malahide papers is of how small a part of Boswell's hectic life, as lawyer, laird, clubman, traveler and lover, was taken up with the great work once considered his exclusive life occupation. The biography was written, it almost now seems, on the fringe of a busy existence.

The old downgrading of Boswell was accompanied by a downgrading of his friendship with Johnson. He was seen as a kind of remora fish attached by the suckers of flattery to a leviathan, occasionally brushed off by the impatient monster of the deep, though more often tolerated, at times half affectionately, but certainly never loved or even much respected. To re-examine, however, the relationship of the two men in terms of Johnson's own expressions of sentiment, as gleaned from *The Life,* the journals and *A Tour of the Hebrides,* is to discover that it was very probably the deepest to which either was ever a partner. And I say this while freely conceding that Boswell at all times cared more for his future biography than he did for its present subject and that Johnson may not have given much thought to his younger friend when he was not actually talking to him or answering one of his letters. But, then, both men had greatly developed egos.

At the famed first meeting of the two in Thomas Davies's bookstore in 1763, when Johnson was fifty-four and Boswell only twenty-three, the younger man was twice snubbed. When he protested that he could not help "coming" from Scotland, Johnson retorted that that was something "a very great many of your countrymen cannot help," and when Boswell ventured to suggest that Garrick would not begrudge the great doctor a ticket for a play, he brought down on his head an even sterner reply: "Sir, I have known David Garrick longer than you have done: and I know no right you have to talk to me on the subject."

It seemed an inauspicious beginning, but it would have taken more than that to check as eager a celebrity seeker as this young Scot. Encouraged by Davies, he dared to call on Johnson a few days later, and when, taking his leave, he apologized for what might have been deemed an intrusion, he received a polite demurrer: "Sir, I am obliged to any man who visits me." After his second call, their leave-taking was even warmer. "Come to me as often as you can," Johnson bade him.

Boswell took him up on his bid. He even ventured to tell his new friend the story of his life. Johnson assured him that he regarded his prospective situation as a Scottish landlord, with many families dependent upon and attached to him, as preferable to that of a rich London merchant or even an English duke. He expressed the hope that they would pass "many evenings, and mornings too, together," and when Boswell departed for his Grand Tour of the Continent, Johnson accompanied him to Harwich to see him off.

On their trip to the port, stopping to dine at an inn, Johnson showed the intimacy already established between them by joshing his younger friend to a "fat, elderly gentlewoman" who happened to be sitting at their table: "He was idle at Edinburgh. His father sent him to Glasgow, where he continued to be idle. He then came to London, where he has been very idle; and now he is going to Utrecht, where he will be as idle as ever."

Johnson even spoke of joining Boswell in Holland, and when the latter expressed the hope that he would not forget him, replied, "Nay, sir, it is more likely you should forget me." Boswell described their parting: "As the vessel put out to sea, I kept my eyes upon him for a considerable time, while he remained rolling his majestic frame in his usual manner; and at last I perceived him walk back into the town, and he disappeared."

The first chapter of their long acquaintance had ended on a note of decided intimacy. Boswell was more than the interviewer; he had told Johnson all about himself and had sought his advice on what to study in Holland and what to see in Europe. And Johnson's interest had been quasi-paternal; there is a sigh of loneliness and age in his speculation that youth may lose sight of him with new distractions.

He need not have worried, however. Nothing was less likely

than that Boswell should lose sight of him. When the latter returned to London in 1766, and on his almost annual trips to the capital from Scotland thereafter, he established the habit of constantly calling upon or dining out with the great man, and in making notes of their conversations, a practice in which he grew so skilled as to become a kind of recording machine. Of course, he had planned from the beginning to make some sort of a printed record of these, but in what form he did not know, and on Johnson's death in 1784 he had still written no part of the great biography.

As one watches Boswell develop his talents of examination and cross-examination, designed to bring out the opinions and passions and even the many violent prejudices of his subject, one has the sense of a venturesome tamer in the cage of a dangerous beast. The animal will respond by performing almost any trick if properly handled, but the trainer may get bitten or mauled in the process. Boswell used the analogy himself on one occasion when he thought he might have gone too far. He had been leading Johnson too persistently into a discussion of the afterlife, a subject that always aroused the greatest dread in his friend.

> I attempted to continue the conversation. He was so provoked that he said: "Give us no more of this," and was thrown into such a state of agitation that he expressed himself in a way that alarmed and disturbed me, showed an impatience that I should leave him, and when I was going away, called to me sternly, "Don't let us meet tomorrow" ... I seemed to myself like the man who put his head into the lion's mouth a great many times with perfect safety, but at last had it bit off.

But of course Boswell called the next day anyway, and Johnson made no reference to the unpleasantness. He became almost immune to Johnson's barbs, which, after all, were grist to his mill, to be carefully recorded, no matter how personal. When he asked Johnson once whether he would not allow a man to drink to forget a disagreeable experience, Johnson retorted, "Yes, Sir, if he sat next *you,*" and on another occasion he exclaimed, "You have but two topics, yourself and me, and I'm sick of both!" Even the great man's compliments were grudging: "Sir, your pronunciation is not offensive" and "I will do to you, Boswell, the justice to say that you are the most unscottified of your countrymen."

But it is not difficult to make out that the relationship was far from one-sided. The tamer *was* making the lion jump through hoops. It was he who arranged the seemingly impossible interview between the ultra-conservative Johnson and the radical John Wilkes and got the two men to talk to each other. Mrs. Thrale said that curiosity carried Boswell further than it ever carried any mortal being. He knew that Johnson, with his fear of death, hated to have his birthday noticed, and he noticed it anyway. On the tour of Scotland he induced one hostess to offer Johnson a cold sheep's head for breakfast to watch the indignant reaction. And when he voiced the wish to see Johnson with a lady he knew the latter detested, he simply jotted down the angry retort: "You would not see us quarrel to make your sport."

The Scottish tour in 1773 brought a change in the relationship. In London Johnson was always the great man and Boswell the visiting Scot. But now for some months Johnson, though still the great man and everywhere greeted as such, was nonetheless a stranger in a land where his friend was an important person and a necessary guide. Even the hardships of travel in rough terrain and the inevitable quarrels deepened their intimacy. In the formidable pass Maam-Ratagain Johnson's horse stumbled and he became seriously alarmed. When Boswell without explanation started to ride ahead to be sure that everything would be in readiness at the inn, Johnson thought he was being deserted, and he recalled him with a great shout. That night he assured Boswell that if he had gone on without him, he would never have spoken to him again after their return to Edinburgh. But that kind of a burst of temper can bring people closer.

There was also on the trip, as Frank Brady, Boswell's biographer, has pointed out, the only example of sexual competitiveness between the two men. Johnson had spoken in jest of how he would clothe the ladies in a seraglio, and when Boswell had laughed at the idea of his having one, he had retorted that, "properly prepared," Boswell would have made a very good eunuch in his establishment. Boswell, stung, had replied that he would play his part better than Johnson, at which the older man had become so nasty that Boswell, for once at last, could not bring himself to record what he had said.

An earlier fantasy of sexual roles had been friendlier. An ugly old crone whose hut Johnson had wished to visit was afraid that the two travelers wished to go to bed with her. Boswell records in *A Tour* how he and Johnson made merry of this afterwards.

> I said it was he who alarmed the poor woman's virtue. "No, Sir," said he. "She'll say, 'There came a wicked young fellow, a wild young dog, who I believe would have ravished me had there not been with him a grave old gentleman who repressed him. But when he gets out of the sight of his tutor, I warrant he'll spare no woman he meets, young or old.'" "No," said I. "She'll say, 'There was a terrible ruffian who would have forced me, had it not been for a gentle mild-looking youth, who, I take it, was an angel.'"

Surely this delightful passage shows a new depth of friendship. It is reminiscent of the scene in *Henry IV, Part I,* where

Prince Hal and Falstaff take turns enacting a fancied discussion between Hal and the king about his fat friend.

After the tour there was a new note of exuberance in Boswell's accounts of his reunions with his friend in London. In 1776 he described his hurrying to Mrs. Thrale's:

> I hastened thither and found Mrs. Thrale and him at breakfast. I was kindly welcomed. In a moment he was in a full glow of conversation, and I felt myself elevated as if brought into another state of being. Mrs. Thrale and I looked to each while he talked, and our looks expressed our congenial admiration and affection for him . . . "There are many [she replied] who admire and respect Mr. Johnson; but you and I *love* him."

Boswell was particularly exuberant on each of these returns, and, as Frank Brady has put it in *James Boswell, the Later Years,* "Johnson is one of the principal keys to Boswell's exuberance, because their love for each other allowed Boswell to approve of and love himself." Yet he could never be sufficiently assured of the great man's regard, which sometimes made Johnson impatient. As he once expressed it to Boswell: "My regard for you is greater almost than I have words to express, but I do not choose to be always repeating it; write it down in the first leaf of your pocket book, and never doubt of it again."

Which is exactly what the literal-minded Boswell did.

He was not in London when Johnson died. He recorded that he was "stunned in a kind of amaze" when he heard that his mind's "great sun" had set. He knew that sorer sensations would come afterwards. That night he made love to his wife.

A few weeks later he dreamed that Johnson was sitting in a chair opposite him in his usual dress.

> He then said in a solemn tone, "It is an awful thing to die." I was fully sensible that he had died some time before, yet had

not the sensation of horror as if in the presence of a ghost. I said to him, "There, Sir, is the difference between us. You have got that happily over." I then felt tenderly affected and tears came into my eyes, and clasping my hands together, I addressed him earnestly, "My dear Sir! Pray for me!" ... God grant us a happy meeting!

And while waiting for that reunion he started on the great book that would make them both live as long as the language.

$\mathcal{E}$DITH WHARTON

and

$\mathcal{M}$ARGARET CHANLER

*A Friendship
of Shared
Good Taste*

$\mathcal{P}$ERCY LUBBOCK, whose brilliant *Portrait of Edith Wharton* is frequently misunderstood as a denigration of the novelist by critics who cannot fathom how deeply he understood the now-departed society in which she moved, and what it meant to her both as an artist and as a woman, purports to explain why she preferred Paris to London. The English way of friendship, however comforting, was "too simple for words"; it took trust and loyalty for granted. Edith may have felt that to prefer it to the more formal and difficult Gallic way was to take life too easily, even to shirk a bit one's puritanically felt duty. Across the Channel the problem of language, the custom of wit, the need to sparkle offered her a challenge to which she leaped, even if it cost her an effort disproportionate to the result.

This effort, according to Lubbock, "was betrayed by her prompt relaxation when the guests had dispersed — when she could quit the stage and throw up her part and say what she liked to her friends. The blessed relief!"

To her "friends"? So they were, after all, English or American. With these, it seemed, she could sit back and be herself. But Lubbock makes it clear that she never sat back very far. She was always shy if never timid.

> *She* was kind, *she* was welcoming and reassuring, if you like — or if *she* liked; but I don't see another consoling her fears by such mild means. The way to her confidence was through free converse, direct communication, open companionship, with all the intimacy that doesn't cling or bind, not more. Is that no intimacy at all? Answers evidently differ; but no friend of hers didn't deeply prize her friendship. There was, to be sure, one other condition to be satisfied in approaching her: you *must* realize that a person in her position has her position to think of — not indeed for a moment that of a woman of celebrated talent, which could easily take care of itself, but that of a lady who, as the poet says, was *such* a lady. Social place must first be recognized, then given its due; and this was always the other little preoccupation in her reception, never quite unguarded, of the thronging world.

Caught in an uncongenial marriage, with no shared tastes but travel, and solaced by a single love affair of brief duration in her middle forties, childless and with no close family ties but one niece and a devoted former sister-in-law, Edith depended on friends for much of the warmth and amusement of life. But she avoided the closest ties. Margaret Chanler has said that whenever an old friend or relative, of either sex, was about to kiss Edith on the cheek, she would place a hand on that person's shoulder as if to check any bestial impulse that might unexpectedly erupt.

Lubbock thought that she felt safer with men, "safer from the claims and demands of a personal relation: from some of which she shrank so instinctively that intimacy, what most people would call intimacy, was to her of the last difficulty."

Lubbock did not go on to point out that there was a slightly epicene quality to the intellectual and sensitive men she chose for her closest friends: Henry James, Howard Sturgis, Logan Pearsall Smith, Robert Norton, Gaillard Lapsley, confirmed bachelors all. And Lubbock himself was evicted from the circle of the elect when he shocked the group by becoming the final husband of Lady Sybil Desart, who had already twice before committed *lèse-majesté* with respect to Edith by marrying her friends Bayard Cutting and Geoffrey Scott.

Intimacy, at any rate, is not essential to even the best friendships. Indeed, too much of it may weigh a friendship down. Edith was always going to guard certain areas of herself from inspection. The nearest I can find that she ever came to deep candor was when she suddenly blurted out to the sympathetic young Frenchman Charles Du Bos, who had translated some of her work, "Ah, the poverty, the miserable poverty of any love that lies outside of marriage, of any love that is not a living together, a sharing of all!" Such a sharing was something, obviously, that Edith had never enjoyed.

She may indeed have been more at her ease with men of the group described than with women, but it was surely harder in her day to find women of her world with the congeniality she sought. I suspect that her formal manners, her "stylishness," would have put off the professional women, and she had a barely concealed disdain for the merely fashionable society types. To find a friend who was as much a "lady" as herself and with comparable taste, education and intellect was no easy task.

Margaret (Daisy) Terry Chanler (Mrs. Winthrop Chanler), however, was to prove just such a one. Edith describes their childhood meeting in Rome in *A Backward Glance:*

But the liveliest hours were those spent with my nurse on the Monte Pincio, where I played with Marion Crawford's little half-sister, Daisy Terry, and her brother Arthur. Other children, long since dim and nameless, flit by as supernumeraries of the band; but only Daisy and her brother have remained alive to me. There we played, dodging in and out among old stone benches, racing, rolling hoops, whirling through skipping ropes, or pausing, out of breath, to watch the toy procession of stately barouches and glossy saddle-horses which, on every fine afternoon of winter, carried the flower of Roman beauty and nobility round and round and round the restricted meanderings of the hill-top.

Daisy in her own memoirs writes that all she could remember of Edith at that early time was "a quantity of long red-gold hair and a smart little sealskin coat, the first I ever saw, and also that she was called 'Pussy,' a name connected in my mind with our big yellow cat, Felicita."

Their next meeting, in Newport, when both were of debutante age, was even less fruitful:

It was there that I met Edith Wharton, then "Pussy" Jones, who was later so vastly to enrich my life with her abounding gift of friendship. We were at a musicale given by Mr. Edward Potter. I had played the piano and accompanied my brother's singing. My father came up to me and said, "I want you to make the acquaintance of Miss Jones, the daughter of one of my best friends." We threaded our way through the crowded rooms to a cosy corner where Miss Jones was holding animated conversation with a young man. The presentation was made with much warmth on my father's part; Miss Jones did not look at all pleased or interested, and I, feeling I had interrupted an amusing, possibly important *tête-à-tête,* made my escape as soon as possible. Edith says she does not remember this at all, but remembers me as one whom she at once felt drawn to, and tells me flattering things about my music. To me she was then just one of the many well-dressed girls with plenty of admirers who made me feel slightly ill at ease.

Their real friendship had to wait for middle age. Daisy, although always internationally minded, spent much of her time when her seven children were growing up in New York, while Edith had finally settled in Paris. Besides, Edith was never much concerned with her friends during their years of domestic preoccupation. Daisy once remarked that if the devil should ever appear to Edith, it would be in the shape of a small child. And there was another factor, their husbands. Daisy had married what she called "a charming idler"; Edith had married simply an idler.

Winthrop Chanler was as intelligent as he was charming, but his first and foremost interest was always in his own amusement. The money was his, and he did not hesitate to dictate just how it should be spent and where and how they would live. When he planned to sell the farm in Geneseo, New York, which had provided Daisy with the only truly adored and seemingly permanent home in her wandering life, because the hunt there was to be discontinued, she protested desperately that hunting wasn't the only thing in life. But he simply retorted, "Well, but you see, for me it is," and "there was nothing more to say." Happily the Geneseo hunt was saved, and so was Daisy's home.

"Winty" had much less use for Edith Wharton than for her books; he said once that the only time he had seen her look pretty was when someone kissed her under a palm tree. Where, I wonder, was that restraining hand? And surely Daisy, like all of Edith's circle, had even less use for Teddy Wharton. It was probably only with Edith's ultimate separation and divorce and with Winty's increased independence from Daisy (he loved to go off on exploring trips with male friends) that the friendship between the two women really flowered, and they began to travel in Europe together. When Edith in 1926 chartered the yacht *Osprey* for an extended cruise in the Mediterranean, she invited Daisy but not Winty. No doubt she knew him well enough to anticipate the high, snotty, Chanler laugh that would have accompanied his description of her ship's company as "bluestockings and dried-up old bachelors."

Teddy Wharton tried to fit into Edith's world but made a pest and fool of himself. Winthrop Chanler had not the slightest need for Daisy's; he was perfectly willing to avail himself of it, on amusing occasions, but any adapting of lives to others would have to be on her part. It made for a much happier marriage than poor Edith's. I believe that Daisy would have gone further to please him had further steps been welcome. As it was, she respected his independence, except when she felt he was directing too much attention to another woman, and then, as she told me once, she interposed her will only to the extent of promptly making friends with the lady in question. Nothing was better calculated to cloud a husband's wandering eye than to see its object arm in arm with his spouse. Queen Alexandra, it is true, had adopted the same policy with little success, but then King Edward, one infers, was a much cruder type than Winty.

In middle age, with Teddy Wharton out of the picture and Daisy's children grown, the two women took great delight in joining forces for the happy game of what Henry James had called "the wear and tear of discrimination." They took what Edith termed "motor flights" together to inspect the great churches, castles and gardens of France and Italy, and when the ocean was between them they exchanged letters about the books they were reading and the interesting people they met.

It seems to one glancing through their correspondence that they were constantly on the go, yet Edith considered the pace of their lives leisurely in contrast to the frenetic activity of youth in the roaring twenties, as she wrote to Daisy in 1923. "Your plans for the winter *must* include a good quiet fortnight *at least* at Hyères [Edith's winter home in the south of France]. The mere description of N.Y. life as practised by the 'youngs' makes me long for my lazy terraces with a jug of Evian, a book, & 'thou' under a caroubier bough!"

It was probably significant in their friendship that Daisy was not an artist. As it was, her life and personality seemed beautifully to complement Edith's. For to Edith her writing, the "secret garden," although kept to its assigned place in her ordered schedule, was still the most vital part of it. Daisy, on the other hand, was never artistically creative, a situation that she freely accepted. When she asked the French artist who was giving her daughter Laura painting lessons what he really thought of the girl's aptitude, and was told that he feared that Laura's fine professional talent would suffer from the "distractions of life," she agreed, but added to herself, "The things of life are the almost inevitable pitfall for a woman's talent, and who should say it is not better so?" These "things" included for herself the raising of seven children and for Laura of eight.

It was said of Daisy that had she been a snob, she would have had a world of types to choose from. She could have been a blood snob: her mother's family, the Wards, were related to everybody in "Old New York," and her aunt Julia had written "The Battle Hymn of the Republic." She could have been a purse snob: her husband, Winthrop Chanler (also her cousin), was an Astor heir. She could have been an international snob: she had been raised in Rome, was fluent in Italian, French and German, and felt as much at home in the capitals where those languages were spoken as in New York. She could have been a music snob: with her expertise at the piano she might have aspired to the concert stage. She could even have been an athletic snob: she hunted the fox in Europe and America until she was in her seventies and took riding lessons from a *haute école* teacher in Paris who trained her in the intricacies of *passage, piaffer* and *pirouette.* And last, but by no means least, she could have been a religious snob: she was the most devout and well instructed of Catholic converts.

But she wasn't a snob. She was simply an ultra-civilized person. Of course, it is often the fate of such to be taken for snobs. It is hard for some to believe that with so many gifts they do not condescend to more ordinary mortals. But I suspect that Daisy believed that her talents were more equalizing than promoting, that her appreciation of beauty in art, music and literature, for example, put her on a kind of par with those who created the beauty. For what would it profit a man to write *Hamlet* to recite it in a desert? Or to compose *Tristan und Isolde* to sing it in the wilderness? The person to whom a *complete* communication could be made had to live on the same level as the communicator.

Art was not only an integral part of Daisy's life; it had even its share in her faith. There were moments when her deepest religious impulses seemed to border on the aesthetic, when we see her in her memoirs leaving a ball in Rome, an opera cloak and black lace mantilla disguising her Paris gown of salmon-pink satin, to attend a pontifical midnight mass at Saint Peter's. "As the liturgical hymn to the Holy Ghost, the beautiful *Veni Creator Spiritus,* floated up amid the clouds of incense into the vast crepuscular dome, the transient self became merged in the transcendent act of worship that must endure *per omnia saecula saeculorum.*"

She was not like her friend Matilda, wife of the painter of charming French interiors, Walter Gay, who defended the hideous private chapel in her beautiful château from Daisy's strictures in this way: "I know it is very bad, but you see I learned to pray in the ugly Catholic churches of old New York, and I do not care for religious aestheticism."

Daisy, raised as a Protestant by expatriate parents in Rome, had found little inspiration in the "converted hay barn" to which the reformed church had been reduced on the Via Flaminia. "The whitewashed walls, the dull hymn singing, the long service were a great weariness to my childish soul." She became an early convert to the older faith.

Daisy's life, as recorded in the two volumes of her memoirs, *Roman Spring* and *Autumn in the Valley,* the latter referring to New York's Genesee Valley, where she and her husband had moved for the fox hunting, was filled to the brim with civilized pleasures. One reader told me that it made him feel all thumbs. Yet it is an impressive account of how one gifted person could make the most of splendid opportunities. Did Daisy, one wonders when turning the pages, ever miss out on anything? Perhaps once. When Franz Liszt asked her to play the piano for him, she had a sprained wrist and could not comply.

But that was unusual. Joseph Rubinstein, the pianist at the original rehearsals for Wagner's great tetralogy in Bayreuth, initiated her into the glories of the Ring. Henry James dubbed her the most cultivated American woman he had known. Henry Adams gave her the unpublished manuscript of his Prayer to the Virgin of Chartres. Theodore Roosevelt ignored precedence to place her next to him at dinner. And she was one of the last to visit the dying former President's bedside. Holding her hand, he had assured her he would get better: "I cannot go without having done something to that old gray skunk in the White House." Nor were her pleasures confined to the intellect. Her home life was happy. Her children grew up to be as brilliant as herself. There seemed no joys not available to her: music, art, literature, friendship, family love, and in the end she had no doubt that an even richer heaven awaited her.

Was it too much? Was her quest of pleasure, even of the most refined sort, a bit excessive? When in a church in Cefalu in Sicily she risked her neck by climbing a three-story-high teetering ladder to get a better glimpse of a mosaic? But I can think of only one incident that she records which really bothers me. She tells how she protected herself from ennui in a New York social season of the early 1890s by inventing a secret insurance company against the disaster of sitting by a bore at dinner. Each member of the little company would present with his or her dues a private list of the most dreaded dinner companions. Then, if one "happened to find oneself again seated beside the flower of them all, there would be the cheering consolation that one could, with the well-earned premium, buy oneself a new hat, a nice engraving, or what not." It seemed to me that this was taking a bit of boredom too seriously. But maybe this was a real part of the keenness of her appetite for pleasure. Certainly, her pleasures were so intense that it was sometimes hard to leave them even for others:

> Early in October I took the whole brood to Europe. My husband stayed behind to get a few weeks of fox hunting in Geneseo before following us across the ocean ... I remember how hard and foolish it seemed to leave the Valley on that last week before we took the night train to New York. Autumn was flaunting its glory of crimson and gold, hanging its banners over the hills and valleys.

Did she ever feel the need to play a more contributing role? I doubt it. I think she felt she was making an adequate contribution by being what she was. "Charming people," she asserted in *Roman Spring,* "are the light and joy of the world."

Charming people, she admits, "have not made history, but their presence in the world made causes worth fighting for, made life worth living, turned the valley of tears into a place of smiles and laughter. It is good to know that such people have always enriched the world with their presence, without trumpet blasts of fame, leaving no tangible masterpieces to testify to their worth. Their masterpiece was their life."

I did not know Mrs. Chanler until the very end of her long life. She had never been a beautiful woman, but there was a wonderful serenity on her long narrow features, in the light steady gaze of her eyes and in her kindly but quizzical half smile. I used to read to her sometimes of a late afternoon, always from Henry James novels of the final, the "major" phase. Her eyes would close, and she would sit so still that I would begin to wonder whether she hadn't drifted off to sleep. But never. In a moment she would raise an interrupting finger and suggest: "Would you mind going over that last sentence again? I think you haven't found the central verb."

Edith wrote to Daisy that when they were apart she kept her "tucked away in my warmest heart valve." But were things always smooth when they were together? Of course not. Mrs. Chanler told me that Edith could be an exasperating traveling companion, impossibly critical of restaurants and hotel accommodations, and that she would be very put out if Daisy was not available for a proposed trip because she had to visit one of her children, drawn by what Edith called "an as yet unsevered umbilical cord."

Daisy, however, took these things in her stride, and I doubt, on her side, serene and patient as she was (even with bores, when she had the bad luck to be with one), that Edith had much to complain of. The mutual understanding and shared tastes of the two women are vividly set out in a letter of

Edith's of 1925 (which Mrs. Chanler gave me and which is now at Yale) about the critical reaction to *A Mother's Recompense.*

> Thank you ever so fondly for taking the trouble to tell me *why* you like my book. Your liking it would be a great joy, but to know why is a subtle consolation for densities of incomprehension which were really beginning to discourage me. No one else has noticed "desolation is a delicate thing," or understood that the key is there. The title causes great perplexity, but several reviewers think it means that the mother was recompensed by "the love of an honest man." One enthusiast thinks it has lifted me to the same height as Galsworthy & another that I am now equal to Scott Fitzgerald. And the Saturday Review (American) critic says I have missed my chance, because the book "ought to have ended tragically" — *ought to!*
> — You will wonder that the priestess of the Life of Reason shd take such things to heart; & I wonder too. I never have minded before; but as my work reaches its close, I feel so sure that it is either nothing, or far more than they know . . . And I wonder, a little desolately, which?
> Like all honest letter writers, I have begun by talking about myself, and having *vidé mon sac* have now time to turn my attention to yours, which was a real horn of plenty — I'm so glad that London was such a success, and that you got hold of the right people and saw the perfect things.

That was the note that binds them: the right people and the perfect things.

Arthur Hallam

and

Alfred Tennyson

A Remembered
Friendship

$\mathcal{B}$ECAUSE OF the fame of *In Memoriam,* the great elegy that Tennyson published in 1851 to commemorate the life and death of Arthur Henry Hallam, the adored companion of his youth, any consideration of friendship in general is bound to touch on the relationship between the two men. Hallam had died of a fever eighteen years before at the age of only twenty-three, and it was long popular in the Victorian era to picture the poet as a kind of lost soul wandering in the valley of despair until healing time, a delayed but happy marriage and the catharsis of putting together the poems that made up his mighty dirge, had brought him to a heroic acceptance of his tragedy. But it later appeared that Tennyson was by no means always in so sorrowful a state, that he was a rather roistering frequenter of taverns, that his poetic silence was occasioned more by a sullen resentment of early critics than by grief and that his long postponement of his nuptials was the result of his largely imaginary fear of a disqualifying epilepsy, his almost wholly imaginary poverty and the slightness of his sexual inclination for the devout and middle-aging Emily Sellwood.

There can be no real doubt, however, of his devotion to Hallam. What is wrong with the picture is the tenacity of the latter's hold — or of the latter's image's hold — on his affections. There is no other example of such depth of feeling for any other human being, male or female, in the poet's long life. Indeed, Tennyson, morbidly self-centered, had little use for people except as mirrors of his own titanic reflection. The mourner of Hallam, like the Hamlet of T. S. Eliot's essay, seems a man "dominated by an emotion which is not expressible because it is in excess of the facts as they appear."

Am I suggesting, then, that had Hallam lived, Tennyson might have tired of his company as he tired of that of J. A. Froude, Edward Fitzgerald, Coventry Patmore, James Spedding and so many others? I am — unless Hallam should have maintained without a break his early high estimate of his friend's genius. For therein, I suggest, lies the clue.

Arthur Hallam has stimulated the interest of generations of critics because so many of his youthful friends who later made their mark in life — in particular, Tennyson and Gladstone — firmly believed that he was the most promising young man of his time. Little enough evidence, it is true, of so brilliant a future exists in the scanty pile of poems and prose that he left, but who would have predicted a great destiny for Abraham Lincoln, or Thackeray, or Tennyson himself — each almost an exact contemporary — had he perished at the same age? After reading the edition of Hallam's writings compiled by Richard Le Gallienne in 1893, I can well imagine his becoming, if not a great poet, perhaps a critic of note, and even, in the Britain of that day, a leader of the House of Commons. For there are signs of nobility of thought and certainly seeds of eloquence scattered through the little volume.

His background was more distinguished than Tennyson's; his father, Henry Hallam, an admired historian, was rich and socially well connected. Arthur went to Eton and to Trinity College, Cambridge (where he met and immediately befriended Tennyson), and traveled widely in France and Italy, mastering modern languages with the same skill he had shown with the dead ones. He had an early passion for English literature, writing tragedies as a boy which dazzled his family and later turning to poetry, but he had an equal enthusiasm for metaphysics and history, and at his death he was reading for the bar. It seems probable that he was planning an early entry into politics.

He must have had great charm. He was good-looking and high-spirited, despite occasional and, alas, justified depressions about his nagging ill health, and he was active in college debates and social life. But what I find most attractive in his picture is that he was apparently devoid of the massive snobbery of his class and era. He saw at once through Tennyson's clumsy, sullen, defensive rustic airs to the deep sensitivity and genius so truculently concealed, and the two became at once inseparable. Friendship was followed by another bond, for Hallam, on a visit to the Tennysons' rectory in Lincolnshire, became engaged to the poet's sister. It was hardly a match to please the worldly Hallams, but Arthur persisted in his love, won his family over and at the time of his death was planning to marry Emily Tennyson.

That Tennyson, who, though large and handsome, was a rough and unsophisticated parson's son from a northern county who had not attended a proper public school, should have been dazzled by the warm affection and frank admiration of so fine and popular a young worldling as Hallam is hardly surprising. One can imagine the quick collapse of his surly wall. But Hallam's winning ways would not alone have captured so permanently the heart of the most egocentric of English bards, the man who would drop a friend for a word of adverse criticism and who used to read his works by the hour to captive audiences of house guests. No, Hallam, to be so loved, had to adore at the Tennysonian shrine.

In his essay "On Some of the Characteristics of Modern Poetry, and on the Lyrical Poems of Alfred Tennyson," Hallam makes considerable sense in his evaluation of the early Romantic poets, Shelley and Keats:

> So vivid was the delight attending the simple exertions of eye and ear, that it became mingled more and more with their trains of active thought, and tended to absorb their whole being into the energy of sense. Other poets *seek* for images to illustrate their conceptions; these men had no need to seek; they lived in a world of images; for the most important and extensive portion of their life consisted in these emotions, which are immediately conversant with sensation.

Such an analysis seems commonplace today, but it was much less so in 1831 for a twenty-one-year-old. When Hallam came to the subject of Tennyson, however, he allowed friendship to carry him to eulogistic extremes that were later to bring down on the head of the unfortunate object of his laudation the full fury of *Blackwood's Magazine.* But at the time Tennyson's vanity must have been tickled indeed when he read of himself: "We think he has more definiteness, and soundness of general conception, than the late Mr. Keats, and is much more free from blemishes of diction and hasty capriccios of fancy."

Nor was this all. Keats, after all, in 1831 was still not generally recognized as a great poet. Tennyson must have deemed his friend closer to the true note when Hallam said of the sixth stanza of Tennyson's "Recollections of the Arabian Nights" that it was as majestic as Milton, and of the twelfth that it was as sublime as Aeschylus!

The Arthur Hallam who had had the perspicacity to appreciate the early genius of Alfred Tennyson, and to predict his great career, had to be shown in *In Memoriam* as tragically deprived of a great career himself, and Tennyson assessed Hallam's missed future with extravagant effusion.

> For can I doubt, who knew thee keen
> In intellect, with force and skill
> To strive, to fashion, to fulfil —
> I doubt not what thou wouldst have been:
>
> A life in civic action warm,
> A soul on highest mission sent,
> A potent voice in Parliament,
> A pillar steadfast in the storm.
>
> Should licensed boldness gather force,
> Becoming, when the time has birth,
> A lever to uplift the earth
> And roll it in another course . . .

What less could have been expected of a youth whose "rapt oration" was eagerly anticipated by his fellow students every time they saw "the God within him light his face"?

In Memoriam is a great poem, or series of poems, in the many sections where the poet's grief for his dead friend has been converted into art. But the purely personal stanzas, such as those just quoted, are banal, and the ones where he refers to Hallam's intended marriage to his sister are almost embarrassing.

> For now the day was drawing on,
> When thou shouldst link thy life with one
> Of mine own house, and boys of thine
>
> Had babbled "Uncle" on my knee . . .

At this point the reader may wonder how even an ego the size of Tennyson's should not have suspected that the following stanza of his great elegy might be taken for true:

> Another answers: "Let him be,
> He loves to make parade of pain,
> That with his piping he may gain
> The praise that comes to constancy."

IVY COMPTON-BURNETT

and

MARGARET JOURDAIN

*I*vy COMPTON-BURNETT created a world in her fiction that seems a strange one to the newcomer, but that gradually, if he will read enough of her novels, begins to seem uncomfortably close to his own. For if the stated background is apt to be a large English country house in the late Victorian era inhabited by a big family of characters who, except when caught in some extraordinary crime, seem to have little to do but argue, often acrimoniously, among themselves, it is really the perfunctory setting for a universal clan. Dame Ivy, to give her the title she so justly earned, was not so much concerned with class or type or period in human events as with the actions and reactions, even the smallest, of human beings placed in constant close conjunction with each other. The term that Nathalie Sarraute, of the French *nouveau roman* school (she considered Dame Ivy one of the greatest of English writers), used to describe these phenomena was "tropisms." A tropism is defined in the dictionary as the tendency of a plant or animal to turn in response to an external stimulus, either by attraction or repulsion. I take this to mean that, in respect to people, it is their reaction, both inward and outward, to what is said to them or what is implied.

Dame Ivy did not see the great passions as necessary subjects of fiction. Indeed, one might say that she did not see the great passions as necessary at all. I infer from her work that she conceived of human beings as more like animals than romantic philosophy would tolerate; that their sexual drive, their sexual jealousy, their anger and their affections are confined to particular times and occasions rather than being of lasting and tempestuous duration. She was not much impressed by human love or even by human hate, both of which she probably felt had been overrated by artists through the ages. In her view we differ from beasts essentially in two respects: in our speech and in our striving for power, and to these her novels are largely addressed. Her characters are locked in constant conflict as to who shall rule the home, and they express their arguments in the concise and limpid prose of La Rochefoucauld.

Having reduced her characters to what she considers their essence—ceaseless aggression and ceaseless defense, always expressed in dialogue—Dame Ivy has little use for the usual furniture of fiction. Her skeletal outlines of mansions, schools and villages are placed against a blank backdrop, as in a modern stage set with minimally suggestive scenery, and her plots, flat and plainly stated, contain echoes of Victorian drama or even melodrama, from such classics as *Jane Eyre* and *Wuthering Heights.*

The rest is talk, wonderful talk. One character says: "Words are all we have," to which another replies: "They are used as if they had some power. And how little they have." But that power is enough for Dame Ivy to create her world. "There would not be any subjects if we had not developed the power of speech," says another of her cast. "They are not really natural."

There is usually in her books one character who tries to dominate the others, a parent or grandparent, at least an older relative. The threatened majority tend to form an opposing, murmuring mass; they huddle together and never take their eyes off their tormentor. Usually, the tyrant is quelled in the end, sometimes by death, sometimes by humiliation at exposed wrongdoing, sometimes even by a change of heart. The younger relatives, united in their devastating wit, are like a flock of crows who take advantage of the daylight to drive off the marauding owl.

Now what does all this have to do with friendship? Simply that it was the one human relationship to which Dame Ivy accorded an unmitigated dignity. And at that she limited herself to friendship among members of her own sex. Intimacy among her male characters is apt to be portrayed as homosexual. And marriage in her novels rarely means a fuller life: "I don't want the things it would be full of," a female character observes. Almost all the family relationships in her books are cloyed with resentments. Love between men and women is tense, precarious and rarely lasting. Even masters and servants are mutually suspicious.

Friendship between women, then, seems to have appeared to Dame Ivy as the nearest that humans could come to a rational and fleshless communication of the spirits. Certainly in her own life such a friendship was the source of her happiness and her art.

Ivy was born in 1884, one of the two large broods of a twice-wed famous doctor, an embattled pioneer of homeopathic medicine, and raised in a big crowded house (such as she would write about) near Brighton. As a young woman she was considered brilliantly intellectual; she went to college and read widely in English letters, but she developed early a taciturn and resolutely independent personality. It does not appear that she took much interest in young men, or in many persons, indeed, outside her family, and on the death of her widowed and despotic mother she took over her control of the household and the real estate in which the Compton-Burnett funds had been invested. Unfortunately, she copied her mother in too many respects, and the four unmarried sisters still at home at last rebelled against the rigidity of her rule and moved to London, leaving Ivy disconsolate and alone. Two of the sisters later committed suicide, which, with the death in the First World War of the brother who seems to have been the one person whom the young Ivy really loved, brought her to a nervous collapse that lasted until her meeting with Margaret Jourdain and their decision to share an apartment in London after the Armistice. The sole literary product of Ivy's first thirty years was an almost unreadable George Eliotish novel, *Dolores,* utterly unlike her later books and which she never thereafter could bear to hear spoken of.

Margaret Jourdain's family, descended from French Huguenots, were poor, socially well connected and brilliant. Her father, a vicar in Derbyshire, was not himself a writer, but all of his seven children were, including Eleanor, who, with Miss C. A. E. Moberly, wrote the sensational and widely read *An Adventure* about their supposed encounter with the ghost of Marie-Antoinette in the garden of the Petit Trianon. Margaret, after a college classical education, came home to live with her widowed mother and write. As Hilary Spurling, author of the splendid biography, *Ivy,* has put it, Margaret, between the years 1903 and 1910, wrote nearly sixty articles "on anything from chintzes to Chinese wallpapers, stump work to samplers, card tables, knife cases, old grates and trunks, cradles, tea pots and royal gloves." She also wrote poetry, translated Horace's odes and made herself an expert on the great English country houses, which (not yet opened to the public by the National Trust) her social connections allowed her to study at first hand. She became known as a national authority on furniture, paneling, plaster carving, embroidery and lace; she was professionally consulted by the most fashionable decorators of London. She was one of the "new women," quite able to support herself emotionally as well as financially without the aid of men. But she never affected masculine airs; on the contrary, she tried to set off her considerable plainness with plumed hats and feather boas and gold chains and to lighten the impact of a brusque personality with wit and vivacity. She enjoyed sophisticated people and parties with good talk and bright, unattached young men; she was what would be called today a "fag hag."

When Ivy and Margaret decided to share a home, Margaret was forty-three and Ivy thirty-five. It is easy to see what Ivy saw in Margaret: a whole new way of life full of new friends and new interests, which, even if she was at first a silent looker-on, was bound to revive and rehabilitate her spirits. It is much less clear what Margaret saw in Ivy, then at the low point in her life, desolate, lonely, unoccupied. It seems probable that Margaret wanted someone to care for; she used to treat Ivy in the early days almost as a child. To have someone always at home when she came in, someone loyal, dependable and quiet, who needed her, may have provided Margaret with just the complement she needed for her busy days in the hard-boiled world of fashionable decoration.

The friends, mostly Margaret's, had little enough use for Ivy in the early years of their shared life. "She was a rather stout middle-class woman who poured out cups of tea for all the young men who came to see Margaret," said the decorator Herman Schrijver. "Ivy had no conversation of any sort or kind in those days." And Margaret was even dubious about the worth of the novels that her friend now began to publish. "Ivy's trash" was her joking term for them. She came in time to take great pride in her friend's accomplishment, but it is rarely an unmixed pleasure to those already possessed of some fame to see themselves surpassed by their nearest and dearest, and a person as dedicated as Margaret to the physical décor of life must have found Ivy's *romans démeublés* a bit on the bare side. Yet their partnership in letters as well as living was soon an accepted fact. Hilary Spurling has described their working habits:

> While Ivy worked at her ease with a notebook on her knees in the drawing room, Margaret wrote all her books in her tiny bedroom on a hard chair pulled up to the dressing table with a litter of notes, cuttings, jottings on old bills and backs of used envelopes spread on the bed.

In time Margaret's work came to have some of the stripped quality of her friend's, as her gaiety of wit was increasingly modified by her dryness of temper. She seemed to have deliberately curbed the ebullient romanticism of her youth and concentrated her mental power on accuracy and precision in her research. According to Spurling, she eliminated from her writing style "any flicker of individuality or ornament," making her books "painfully skimpy and dull." She despised "the frailty and potential fallibility involved in offering to assess or draw conclusions from original research."

We have seen the events that caused the bitterness in Ivy. She now converted them into art. Her fictional tyrants were in part modeled on her old self. If there was a similar bitterness in Margaret's life, as seems probable, we do not know of it. But there was no bitterness towards each other. Spurling writes:

> In later life they had settled into the comfortable, often captious intimacy of an old married couple. Margaret always re-

mained the active partner, the forceful, enterprising, in some ways masculine one of the two, though . . . their oldest friends agreed that it was frankly preposterous to picture Ivy and Margaret as lovers . . . But her feeling for Ivy was deep, constant and grounded in that rush of fierce, anxious tenderness that any sign of strain in Ivy . . . could always evoke in her friend. It explains Ivy's unexpected dependence on Margaret as well as the dominance over her noted by so many of their visitors: the fact that, though Ivy was the housekeeper, the one who poured tea and dealt with the tradespeople, she was also the one who needed to be looked after.

That Margaret provided an actual model for Ivy to emulate in her fiction is borne out by an early friend of the two, Raisley Moorsom, who said: "Margaret talked like a character out of Ivy's books. Ivy couldn't do it then [before the friendship]. In the end she learned to talk like one of her own characters."

James Lees Milne, an officer of the National Trust and a friend and co-worker of Margaret's, has vividly recorded his first meeting with Ivy in his World War II diary:

Margaret Jourdain is patently jealous of Ivy Compton-Burnett, whom she keeps unapproachable except through herself, and even when approached, guards with anxious care. This is evident from the way in which the former diverts one's attention if she thinks one is talking too much to the latter. It is a selfish kind of affection, to say the least. The two have lived together for years and are never parted. They are an Edwardian and remarkably acidulated pair. The coiffures of both look like wigs. The hair is bound with a thin fillet across the forehead and over a bun at the back. Thin pads of hair hang down their foreheads unconvincingly. Miss C.-B., whom I consider to be the greatest living novelist, is upright, starchy, forthright and about fifty-seven to sixty. There is a bubbling undercurrent of humour in every observation she makes, and

she makes a good many, apparently hackneyed and usually
sharp, in a rapid, choppy, rather old-fashioned upper-middle-
class manner, clipping her breathless words. She enunciates
clearly and faultlessly, saying slightly shocking things in a
matter-of-fact tone, following up her sentences with a lot of
"dontcherknows," and then smiling perceptibly. She has a
low, breasty chuckle. She has not unpleasing, sharp features,
and her profile is almost beautiful.

When Margaret was dying of heart disease in 1950, all the
long-suppressed tyrant in Ivy came back with her terror of
losing her friend, and the two quarreled grotesquely. But it
was a brief if appalling period, and one imagines that Margaret
understood what Ivy was going through. "Don't let Day [the
maid] eat all the Evas plums," were her final words to her
friend when she was taken off at last to the hospital to die.

Ivy's life fell apart with her loss, but in time she managed to
patch it together, and she emerged a more mellowed character,
passively enjoying her continuing fame and new honors. The
gap, however, was always there. When Lees Milne asked her,
fifteen years after Margaret's death, if she still missed her, Ivy's
grave reply was "Every minute of every day." And when she
was made a Dame of the British Empire, she wrote to a con-
gratulating friend, "I am not fully a Dame, as *she* does not
know about it."

*H*ENRY ADAMS

and

*J*OHN HAY

*I*F ONE COULD CHOOSE, among the eyes of the American past, the pair that had enjoyed the most privileged views of some of our great men, those of John Hay would be a likely selection. To have been the private secretary and daily companion of Abraham Lincoln during the war years, actually living much of that time in the White House, might seem enough in itself, but Hay was also Henry Adams's most intimate friend and, in the early days of the new American imperialism, Theodore Roosevelt's Secretary of State. That his sympathy and understanding must have been large is further evidenced by his closeness to two such diverse Americans as Henry James and William McKinley.

Yet the man who attracted the confidence of titans does not appear to have been one himself. Of course, this may have been one of the reasons. According to his biographer, Tyler Dennett, Hay was "a conventional man, punctilious in dress, careful to observe even the trivial rules of society," one "who shunned extremes and devoted himself to respectability." The son of a country doctor in Indiana, in a day when that was not far from the frontier, he always looked more to the East than to the West and was enchanted to escape to the more cultivated atmosphere of Brown College, where he could read poetry and aspire to be a writer. But for all his romanticism, he kept one foot firmly on the ground, and, after graduating, decided that the bar would be a surer source of support than letters. It was while reading law in his uncle's firm in Springfield, Illinois, that he met John Nicolay, who would shortly be named secretary to the President-elect and take Hay, aged twenty-three, to Washington as his junior.

What would his life have been otherwise? He would still, no doubt, have been a minor poet and a very minor novelist; he might still have married the Cleveland heiress Clara Stone and have succeeded at the bar or even in diplomacy, but it is unlikely that he would have risen to be ambassador to England and Secretary of State without the aura cast by his and Nicolay's great ten-volume life of Lincoln. It is true that this work lacked the intimate touches supplied by biographers of a less formal historical school, and the picture of Lincoln is somewhat conventional and one-sided, but it remains the first great and indispensable document in the long process of the apotheosis of the emancipator. Henry Adams was to decline an honorary degree from Harvard on the ground that he could not countenance "the idea that any work of mine compared in importance either of purpose, of moral value or of public interest to the singularly noble and American character of this monument to the greatest man of our time."

Lincoln was hardly the type of statesman that Hay would have picked for his hero in his Brown days. He would have been more apt to picture one like Gladstone: a polished gentleman, a scholar, an orator of the old school, a born leader who looked every inch the part. But what must be remembered about Hay is that, for all his undoubted worldliness, he had the warmest of hearts and a shrewd and penetrating eye, which could see quality under any guise. He soon came to love the boss whom he referred to privately as "the tycoon" or "the ancient" and about whom he wrote in his diary in 1863:

> The tycoon is in fine whack. I have rarely seen him more serene and busy. He is managing the war, the draft, foreign relations, and planning a reconstruction of the Union, all at once. I never knew with what tyrannous authority he rules the Cabinet, till now . . . There is no man in the country so wise, so gentle, and so firm. I believe the hand of God placed him where he is.

Hay knew that he never would meet Lincoln's like again. As Dennett put it: "Never after Lincoln's death did he choose to associate with any man who remotely resembled the President either in externals or in the more subtle qualities of his character."

Few would have predicted that three decades after the assassination Hay would become Secretary of State. Although always active in politics, he never showed ambition for the highest offices. He served in Paris immediately after the war as secretary of the legation and then abandoned diplomacy for journalism. After his marriage to the daughter of the wealthy Cleveland railway magnate Amasa Stone, he went for a time into business with his father-in-law, continuing to write on the side and publishing anonymously in 1881 a novel, *The Bread-Winners,* which demonstrated that he was heart and soul on the side of the great industrialists into whose midst he had wed. For in this tale the radical and malicious strikers in a city that is obviously Cleveland are successfully foiled by the heroic action of a rich and cultivated war veteran, who has also attempted to water his arid home town with the blessings of European art.

In 1879 Hay's loyal support of the Republican Party was

rewarded by his appointment as Assistant Secretary of State by the Ohioan Rutherford B. Hayes, a post he held for a year and a half and which involved a welcome return to Washington and to a social life far more delectable than any provided by Euclid Avenue. Hay decided to remain in the capital with his family after he left office, entertaining the great and near-great in their mansion on Lafayette Square and spending his days at work on the life of Lincoln, which would not be published until 1890.

Washington brought friendship with Henry and Clover Adams. Adams and Hay had met as far back as 1861, when Adams was briefly in Washington as his father's secretary before accompanying him to his post in London, but their intimacy dated from the eighties. The Adamses had no official position in the capital and sought none; they had come down from Boston to be near the National Archives, needed by Henry for his great work on the administrations of Jefferson and Madison, but also to observe, with interest, amusement and derision, the passing parade. The spectacle of the present, matched with the study of the past, provided the historian with a kind of continuous march of folly. Henry and Clover were well qualified to be popular hosts of carefully chosen little dinner parties: they were rich and, genealogically speaking, almost royal; they were acutely intelligent as well as witty, and, having no axe to grind, they could exclude even the mightiest bores at will. Their friend Henry James, modeling a couple on them in a short story written after a visit to the capital, had the wife exclaim, at the end of a social season: "Hang it, there's only a month left, let us be vulgar and have some fun — let us invite the President!"

One can see that Henry may have been everything the young Hay at Brown had aspired to be: the exquisitely cultivated, widely traveled scholar and writer, the man of the world who knew both how to enjoy society and when to scorn it.

Adams had always had money; he could take it for granted and marry the woman of his choice, who had all his wit and far more gaiety and charm. Hay loved his Clara, but she was pious and stout; Adams was to refer in *The Education* to "John Hay, Whitelaw Reid and William C. Whitney, all of whom owed their free hand to marriage, education serving only for ornament." And then, too, it was already evident from Adams's early work, from his essays, his lives of Gallatin and Randolph, his anonymously published novel *Democracy* and from the chapters of his great work in progress, which he showed to Hay, that he was an incomparable master of prose style. It must have sometimes seemed to Hay that the only advantage he had over his friend was Abraham Lincoln, and even there Adams could point to a presidential grandsire and great-grandsire and to having been taken to the White House to meet Zachary Taylor at the age of twelve.

Hay was remarkably modest, and I believe that even as Secretary of State he considered Adams the bigger man. Indeed, I do not think he ever considered himself a great man at all, and in this Adams agreed with him. Writing to an English friend in 1882, he had this to say of Hay:

> He has everything the world can give except strength. He is amiable and clever, and the only fault I have to find with him is that in politics he has always managed to keep in what I think precious bad company. I never could understand why, except that I never knew more than two or three men born west of the Alleghenies who knew the difference between a gentleman and a swindler. This curious obliquity makes him a particularly charming companion to me, as he knows intimately scores of men whom I would not touch with a pole, but who are more amusing than my own crowd.

Of course Hay's usefulness to Adams in providing that eternal *voyeur* of domestic and international politics with a watching post behind the scenes was to multiply itself many times over when he at last entered the Cabinet, and it has caused some critics to see Adams as succumbing to the natural impulse to denigrate a friend who had acted where he had only spied. But I cannot find any evidence of such smallness in Adams's nature. He might have succeeded Hay as ambassador to England when the latter was elevated to State by giving the nod to the many important persons who wanted him. But Adams was always perfectly consistent in refusing to take any official position, and I don't believe that his small opinion of those that did was dictated by envy. He had an equally small opinion of those who, like himself, stood aside to watch. His habit, as Justice Holmes put it, of "posing as the old cardinal who would turn everything into dust and ashes" reflected a sincerely held philosophy.

The friendship, once established, had to be something more than symbiosis — Adams profiting by Hay's political connections and Hay by Adams's great mind and social position — though symbiosis was certainly in it. For if Adams's intimacies were few, they were correspondingly deep and abiding. "One friendship in a lifetime is much," he wrote in *The Education;* "two are many, three are hardly possible." Certainly his two were Hay and Clarence King, the geologist and explorer, a colorful and adventurous character who appealed to the romantic side of both Hay's and Adams's natures, but whose unconventional private life (he was secretly married to a black woman) and constant travels set him somewhat apart from them. King, together with the Hayses and Adamses, made up a secret society dubbed "the Five of Hearts," but with King's absences and Clara Hay's silences, the essential intimacy was between the other three.

The ghastly shock of Clover Adams's suicide in 1885 in a

black fit of depression over her father's death drew the remaining two even closer. Hay wrote to Adams: "I can neither talk to you nor remain silent. The darkness in which you walk has its shadow for me also. You and your wife were more to me than any other two. I came to Washington because you were there."

Indeed, in the year before the tragedy the Adamses and Hayses had built adjoining houses on Lafayette Square, designed by Henry H. Richardson, with handsome, dark red brick Romanesque façades. The two men's constant need of and delight in each other's company, interrupted only by the world wanderings of the disconsolate widower and Hay's post abroad, lasted until Hay's death, in 1905. If there were any fallings-out, they are not recorded in the correspondence, where Adams salutes Hay with such whimsically affectionate terms as "My son John," "Precious Jewel," "Sweet Heart," "Dear Heart" and "Dearly Beloved," and Hay reciprocates with "My one and ownliest," "My Beloved Mentor" and "My Cherished Livy."

With Adams's abandonment of large social gatherings after 1885 (he remained available to a small, chosen circle), Hay, always more at home in the great world, became increasingly his eyes and ears. Adams's romantic retreat to a precapitalist past, to a medieval world where "goldbugs" were replaced by martial barons and cathedral building clerics, where great art could flourish to the clash of swords rather than the chink of coins, was now complemented by his friend's involvement with bargains made in smoke-filled chambers and compromises struck behind the closed doors of European chancelleries. Between them, the two friends managed to cover a wide scope of human thought and human experience. Their strong mutual affection we see reflected in Hay's description of his sometimes too critical friend as an angelic porcupine, and Ad-

ams's joking appeal to Hay, then absent from the capital, to
come back because "I can't run this city alone."

Hay did not altogether share Adams's love of faraway, ex-
otic places and wildernesses, nor did his full family life (Clara
and four children whom he adored) permit him to accompany
his friend on such jaunts, but he made one exception for a
rugged trip to Wyoming, where his conduct aroused Adams's
greatest admiration:

> Hay, who is always the best of companions, and who always
> looks forward with hope to ultimate return to his family, takes
> things better than I do, and, while got up as a land-pirate,
> endures cold feet and cold nose with a grace and humor which
> I would be glad to imitate . . . We have ridden three or four
> hundred miles on ponies through trails or trailless country,
> over mountains and in canyons, sliding on snow or bogged in
> swamp, making twenty-two different camps, with beautiful
> weather and violent thunder-storms, occasional accidents and
> tolerable appetite, living on elk-meat and trout, and threading
> vast forests, until Hay has become a blooming mountaineer,
> and I remain a dude.

Yet for all Adams's devotion to his friend, the self-pity that
creeps out from behind the stern mask of his stoicism occasionally sapped the quantity of his sympathy for others. On the
death of Hay's brilliant son Del, in a freak accident at a Harvard reunion, he could write to Clara Hay:

> As a matter of medical opinion, I should say that I was not
> altogether the best sort of help or tonic to persons needing
> strength and courage. It is so long that I have got the habit of
> thinking that nothing is worth while! That sort of habit is
> catching, and I should not like to risk too close contact at a
> critical moment with a mind disposed to be affected by it.

What a way to stretch out a hand! But Adams's friends always made allowances for his supposedly greater grief.

The heyday of the friendship came when Hay, sixty years of age and already ailing, became Secretary of State for William McKinley and, two years later, for Theodore Roosevelt. The problem for the friends was how to preserve their intimacy without its appearing to be an intrusion on Hay's independence of judgment. That an appearance would be all it was, both were confident. Adams, who had a horror of responsibility, had no desire to be a grey eminence or to direct the administration's foreign policy — of which he anyway disapproved — and most historians of the period agree that his influence on Hay was small. He preferred his role of "twelfth-century monk," and told his friend to let his congratulations "have only the value of a Latin epitaph at the base of your bronze equestrian statue in Roman armor and a laurel wreath."

But Hay would not forgo the comfort and inspiration of Adams's conversation, and it was agreed that they should meet on a daily basis, as described by Adams to Mrs. Dan Cameron, the woman who came nearest (which was not too near) to replacing Clover in his constant need for female companionship and affection:

> At four o'clock Hay generally comes for a walk, and we tramp to the end of 16th Street discussing the day's work at home and abroad. Then at five we get back to Mrs. Hay's tea, where someone, agreeable or otherwise, generally drops in. About six I return to my den and close my day . . . To refuse him my help would be most disagreeable to me; but to accept office would be misery. What I like — for I am, as you have often said, a mass of affectation and vanity — is to have people make me pretty speeches, which they do, and to grin behind their backs, as they do behind mine.

We shall never know just what the two friends discussed on that daily hour-long walk, but I suspect that what Adams wisely provided for his harassed friend was the chance to sound off about the obtuseness of senators and the misery of trying to form a coherent foreign policy with so many interested eyes peering over his shoulder. And when he talked in turn I imagine it was to put the frustrating day into its historical perspective and ease the nerves of the ailing and perturbed public servant with a sense of how small a part it was of a probably senseless infinity. "We survey the universe with a daily observation," Adams observed.

Adams personally had little enthusiasm for the new imperialism of American policy under McKinley and Roosevelt; he favored the establishment of United States economic and consequent political influence over the two Americas and disapproved of involvement in the Philippines and China. Also, he regarded Hay as hopelessly at the beck and call of two imperious Presidents. When he was away from Washington a more critical note crept into his letters to his friend. "Your open door is already off its hinges," he wrote to him of his China policy from Paris in the summer of 1900. "What kind of a door can you rig up? Oh, but I don't want to get into it! The twelfth century is good enough for me."

But he gave Hay some rather grudging praise in the following fall when the problem of the Boxer Rebellion seemed to have been worked out:

> In watching you herd your drove of pigs, I am at times astonished to see how, by hitting one on the snout and by coaxing another with a rotten turnip, you manage to get ahead, or at least not much backward; but this is not the kind of astonishment I mean. True, your success has been surprising. You have been so right when everybody else was wrong, that I half believe you are too good to drive hogs; if anybody can be too

good for a useful purpose. Not that I can even yet see how you mean to herd your swine, or how you go; but I have sublime confidence in time, or perhaps you can get yourself out, even if you leave them in the mire they are so happy to roll in.

By the end of 1900, however, Adams was seriously concerned with Hay's health, and he wrote to Mrs. Cameron:

After watching Hay's condition for three weeks I am regretfully compelled to admit that he must go out or die. His strength is exhausted and his temper too. Whether he will recover must depend, I suppose, on rest and constitution; but for the present he is done. So much of Hay's valetudinarianism has always been nervous that I fully admit he may live to be ninety; but he is no longer fit to be Secretary. *Enfin,* he is writing his resignation.

But four days later the situation had changed.

Hay is about again, after a fashion. His case is particularly complicated. He does not know whether his *angina pectoris* or his *angina senatus* is more serious. Whether he has organic trouble with his heart, I do not know, nor as yet does he, but he certainly has organic trouble with the Senate. It is the old story of cutting cheese with a razor. Hay was made to be a first-rate ambassador abroad; he loathes being a third-rate politician at home.

Adams's opinion was to some degree shared by Theodore Roosevelt, a younger friend but hardly an admirer of both men. Early in the new President's administration, in January of 1902, Adams wrote to Mrs. Cameron, after a dinner at the White House at which both he and the Hays had been guests:

One condition is clear. Hay and I are shoved to a distinct seniority; we are sages. I feel it not only in Hay's manner, but in Roosevelt's too, and it is my creed now that my generation had better scuttle gracefully, and leave Theodore to surround himself with his own Rough Riders.

In 1909, four years after Hay's death while Roosevelt was still in office, the President was displeased by a selection of Hay's letters published by his widow. He was particularly disgusted to learn that Hay had written in 1902 a letter of congratulation to Prime Minister Balfour on his "accession to the most important official post known to modern history"! TR wrote to Henry Cabot Lodge:

> But he was not a great secretary of state . . . He had a very ease-loving nature and a moral timidity which made him shrink from all that was rough in life, and therefore from practical affairs. He was at his best at the dinner table or in a drawing room, and in neither place have I seen anyone's best that was better than his. But his temptation was to associate as far as possible with men of refined and cultivated tastes, who lived apart from the world of affairs, and who, if Americans, were wholly lacking in robustness of fibre.

In another letter the Rough Rider made it clear that his reference to these men of taste included particularly Henry Adams.

Adams, as had become his custom, was spending the summer in Paris when Hay died on July 1, 1905. He wrote to Mrs. Cameron:

> You were more shocked than I, and for the reason that I am so tiresome about preaching. I am a pessimist — dark and deep — who always expects the worst and is not surprised

when it comes. Hay was by nature another, but never in his life had a misfortune or unhappiness till Del's death. Both of us knew, when we parted, that his life was ended, and that the mere day or month or year of actual death was a detail. We had been discussing it for at least two years. Naturally it surprised neither of us.

But to Margaret Chanler he wrote:

I am isolated, superannuated, senile and silent. I have to bottle up my most effervescent antipathies, and am bored to suicide; but I am going on to run the machine alone since my last ally has had his life crushed out of him by it.

HENRY JAMES

and

FRIENDSHIP

$\mathcal{H}$ENRY JAMES was an immensely gregarious man who, at least in his younger years, made a point of meeting everyone of note in the great cities that he visited or in which he resided: New York, Boston, Washington, London, Paris, Rome. During the London winter of 1878–1879 the engagement book of this popular thirty-five-year-old bachelor records his dining out a hundred and forty times. His hosts were not only writers, publishers and journalists; they included politicians, soldiers, scientists, painters, sculptors and architects. He seems to have been determined to penetrate to the very heart of British society.

As a young lawyer in the late 1940s I assisted in the administration of the estate of his nephew, also Henry James, who had inherited Lamb House, his uncle's residence in Rye, and whose widow decided to deed it to the National Trust. But the library she sold to a book dealer in Rye for $750. When I, a devoted Jacobite, protested in horror, she insisted that her husband had already given his uncle's valuable books to Harvard. But he hadn't. Those shelves were laden with presentation copies of first editions affectionately inscribed by some of the most important writers in Europe and America. That book dealer made a killing.

James's acquaintances in the literary world were not superficial. He was a close friend of Stevenson, Howells, Daudet, Conrad, Wharton, Welles, Walpole, Gosse — the list could go on and on. He was an open-armed, welcoming host, an almost overappreciative guest, always full of solicitation and smiling good wishes, intensely sympathetic about people's troubles and the most faithful of epistolarians. Leon Edel's edition of his selected letters runs to four fat volumes, and a sizable portion of the text is taken up with James's elaborate apologies for being such a poor correspondent! But the careful reader will detect that under the glorious running style, liberated, almost comically, from the discipline of his art, behind the hyperbole of his constantly (sometimes wearisomely) reiterated expressions of affection ("the mere twaddle of graciousness"), there lurks a certain consistent reserve. James gave much of himself to his friends, but he always held back more than he gave. In the last analysis he valued companionship more than friendship.

This of course is true of many great artists. James's passion for his own creative talent took up the larger part of his large heart. The very exaggeration of his terms of fondness in his letters seems to contain a hint of guilt that he doesn't feel more strongly. Or is he even trying to make a joke of it? Consider this passage in a letter to Edith Wharton about his hoping to see their common friend, Walter Berry, before the latter left to take up a legal post in Egypt:

> If I were only young and gracile, like himself and yourself, only inkless and faithless and tactless, I would dog his very steps before I would let him return to the shining East alone. I

hoped for him here on his way and have been feeling for him
in darkness and storm, please tell him, with a fear that he
would pass and deny me. However, I daresay that he passed 500
miles off, and I only miss him and admire him and bewail him.

One hardly imagines that the writer of this effusion lost
much sleep waiting up for Berry or even that he expected his
correspondent to believe that he would. But contrast this with
the note of intimacy in the notebooks, where James croons to
himself over his recovery from the disaster of his theatrical
efforts and discusses with his "Genius" his return to the truer
path of fiction.

> *Causons, causons mon bon* — oh, celestial, soothing, sanctifying
> process, with all the high sane forces of the sacred time fighting
> through it, on my side! . . . I seem to emerge from these recent
> bad days — the fruit of blind accident — and the prospect
> clears and flushes, and my poor blest old Genius pats me so
> admirably and lovingly on the back that I turn, I screw around,
> and bend my lips to passionately, in my gratitude, kiss its hand.

The fact that the letters grow longer and more frequent
with the years may indicate that James was almost as contented
to write to his friends as to see them. He had now accumulated
all the observations that he needed for his fiction (at least until
his return to America in 1904 gave him a fresh crop), and he
found that social life made costly inroads in his writing time.
Holed up more and more in his adored Lamb House, he did
not turn his attention to his friends until late at night — his
time for correspondence, often extending into the small hours
— when he would cover page after page with ideas and reactions and inquiries, combining in this way the art of the writer
with his sympathy for a fellow being, and thus, perhaps, en-
deavoring to persuade his "blest Genius" that he was not even
momentarily forsaking it.

I think that James sounded the deepest notes of the kind of feeling that he had to offer in his description of the last years of Minnie Temple in *Notes of a Son and Brother* and in his correspondence with Edith Wharton. He was certainly not in love with either woman, though he may have wanted to be with Minnie, and, as I have suggested, the term "friendship" had with him a limited significance.

Minnie (Mary Temple) was Henry's first cousin, the daughter of his father's sister, Catherine James Temple. The Temples lived in Albany, but after the premature deaths of both parents, the four young daughters were moved about to the homes of relatives in Newport, in Pelham, New York, in Boston and in North Conway, New Hampshire. It was in North Conway, in the White Mountains, in the summer of 1865, with the terrible war over at last, that Henry had his most glowing memories of Minnie at her brightest and best, surrounded by a circle of admiring and brilliant young men that included himself and his brother William, O. W. Holmes, Jr., and John Chipman Gray, the future Harvard Law professor. James thought of their group in that halcyon season "as having formed a little world of easy and happy interchange, of unrestricted and yet all so instinctively sane and secure association and conversation, with all its liberties and delicacies, all its mirth and its earnestness protected and directed so much more from within than from without" and wondered whether anything like it could exist in the more complicated day (1913) in which he was describing it. But poor Minnie probably already bore the seeds of the consumption that would kill her five years later.

It is difficult to know, as it was difficult for James to know, whether he was able to see Minnie apart from her doom, whether even his earliest memories of her, long before the advent of her fatal illness, were not suffused with the glow of her tragedy. Certainly that glow irradiated her last letters to John Gray, which the latter, four and a half decades later, sent to James to be incorporated in the second volume of his memoirs. James, trying to sum up Minnie in the beginning of the section where these letters were used, saw her as

> absolutely afraid of nothing she might come to by living with enough sincerity and enough wonder ... The charming, irresistible fact was that one had never seen a creature with such lightness of forms, a lightness all her own, so inconsequently grave at the core, or any asker of endless questions with such apparent lapses of care.

Minnie was devoted to James — one sees that in all her references to him and in her letters to him — but her attitude was amused, admiring, cousinly, kind. I cannot help suspecting that she knew he would have liked to be in love with her, and let him, ever so lightly, ever so charmingly, off the hook.

With Gray it was altogether different. He was a very serious young man who seems to have scolded her, even in the last stages of her illness, for not taking a greater interest in intellectual matters. But I think he loved her. James found in their correspondence only the "special quietude" and "high consideration" of a "confident friendship," but I read it otherwise. I am sure that Minnie loved the sober law student to whom she confided her agonizing doubts in the Christian God of whose heavenly kingdom she was so soon to have need. She went to hear the sermons of Phillips Brooks, whom she and Gray both deeply admired, and found that he didn't "touch the real difficulties at all." He was too busy leading his flock to have time to illuminate them, and she felt sadly "run down" and wanted "to see some honest old pagan and shake him by the hand." Her doubts now became terrible.

Can you understand the utter weariness of thinking about one thing all the time, so that when you wake up in the morning consciousness comes back with a sigh of "Oh, yes, here it is again; another day of doubting and worrying, hoping and fearing has begun."

Death "at the last was dreadful to her," James wrote in *Notes to a Son and Brother;* "she would have given anything to live." Her ghost would be with him for years, until he could lay it "in the beauty and dignity of art."

"Dead," Leon Edel has written, "Minnie was Henry's, within the crystal walls of his mind ... He did not have to marry Minnie and risk the awful consequences — and no one else could ... Minnie was now permanently his, the creature of his dreams."

That sounds cold, even heartless, but Edel has perfectly described the artistic process. Twenty-four years after the death of Minnie Temple, James could write in his notebook:

Isn't perhaps something to be made of the idea that came to me some time ago and that I have not hitherto made any note of — the little idea of the situation of some young creature (it seems to me preferably a woman, but of this I'm not sure) who, at 20, on the threshold of a life that has seemed boundless, is suddenly condemned to death (by consumption, heart disease, or whatever) by the voice of the physician? She learns that she has but a short time to live, and she rebels, she is terrified, she cries out in her anguish, her tragic young despair. She is in love with life, her dreams of it have been immense, and she clings to it with passion, with supplication. "I don't want to die — I won't, I won't, oh, let me live; oh, save me!" ... If she only could live just a little; just a little more — just a little longer.

And *The Wings of the Dove* is born.

·   ·   ·

Lyall H. Powers, the editor of James's letters to Edith Wharton, has written that James's association with her love affair with Morton Fullerton — he was the confidant of her scheme to pay off Fullerton's blackmailing ex-mistress — gave him "a good deal of stimulation and gratification" and completed their relationship: "That relationship — the marriage of true minds, sympathetic companionship, frank and intimate confidence and trust — was rounded out by the safely controlled but invigorating element of the erotic."

I find that I cannot agree with this. Of course, these matters are highly speculative, but my impression from James's work and correspondence, and from what has been written of his life, is of a man whose attraction to women had been paralyzed by some early psychic experience and whose mild homoerotic feelings for young men did not develop until his later years — a not uncommon phenomenon in males of previously heterosexual inclinations. If he was attracted to his own sex in his youth and middle years, I know of no evidence of it. It seems quite possible to me that he was attracted to Minnie Temple and very likely to other young women, but was checked from giving his feelings any expression for the reason noted. What does not seem likely to me is that he should ever have been in the least attracted to Edith Wharton or titillated by her sex life. The type of woman who charmed him was the type of Minnie Temple, as exemplified in his heroine Isabel Archer: beautiful, fresh, young, daringly honest and frank, essentially American. Edith, for all her brilliance, erudition and genius, for all her high style and international sophistication, was still something of a plain, bossy bluestocking with an appalling amount of energy. She could never have been a lover in James's daydreams.

She was a friend, of course, and in time she would become the closest friend of his lifetime. But for a long while she was a friend on the same terms as Percy Lubbock and Walter Berry and received letters filled with the same hyperbolic expressions of affection.

"Your letters come into my damp desert here even as the odour of promiscuous spices or the flavour of lucent syrups tinct with cinnamon might be wafted to some compromised oasis from a caravan of the Arabian nights" is the opening of an epistle to her in 1909. And this is his acknowledgment of a gift of fruit:

> This very hour — as I sit here solitudinous — there has dropped upon me a basket, or casket, of celestial manna that can only have been propelled to its extraordinarily effective descent by the very tenderest and firmest, most generous and most unerring hand in all this otherwise muddled world. You are truly of a gorgeousness of goodness . . . I bow my head even while I open my mouth.

He loved to exchange gossip with her about the many friends they shared, and opinions about books and plays. He reveled in the brittle give-and-take of her conversation and delighted in her pose as the most devoted of his disciples, probably never discovering how little she valued the great novels of his late period. And he welcomed her settling in France, in part that he might have the advantage of her "wondrous" automobiles for "motor flights." But he wanted to go only on occasions of his own choosing, and here he ran into a will quite the equal of his own. In time he grew to be a little bit afraid of her, afraid of her sudden raids into his rustic life of quiet creativity, her picking him up, so to speak, and whirling him away on distracting jaunts. His letters to other friends are filled with semihumorous references to "the angel of devastation."

He sought at last to establish a relationship in which she would accept him as a friend whose function was more to

receive than to give, more to sit home and await the news of
her braver flights than to accompany her on them.

> And I have no scruple of saying this to you — your beautiful
> genius being so for great globe-adventures and putting girdles
> round the earth. Mine is, incomparably, for brooding like the
> Hen, whom I differ from but by a syllable in designation.

His role would be to hold out his "now empty cup —
scoured quite clean of baser matter — for whole rich and thick
flowing reports of everything." He would simply lie stretched,
"a faithful old veteran slave on the doormat of your palace of
adventure."

Her invitations, however, continued to be importunate.
Edith could be an imperious friend. She imperiled her relations with Bernard Berenson by objecting too vociferously to the
old man's postprandial naps, which interfered with her afternoon plans when he stayed with her. James had at last, in 1912,
to take a firm stand: "It is written, dearest Edith (and I myself
have written it twenty times, I think), that I shall never (D.V.)
again leave the shores of this island, which makes, I agree, a
dismal enough prospect in respect to seeing you again."

But now his health began seriously to fail. Details, even
rather grotesque ones, made their appearance in his letters to
her. In 1913 he wrote:

> When my accurst Herpes was by the law of Nature beginning
> to be ready to abate, there took place what I believe often
> occurs after a bad career of the complaint, the determination
> of a hideous condition of excruciating pain, horrible chronic
> sore flatulent distention, produced by the neuralgic poison, in
> all the neighbouring stomachic and abdominal tract.

He protests that his social life has now been reduced to
almost nothing: "I practically never dine out and never, never,

never lunch." Yet his engagement book shows that he lunched out five times in two months at just this period. What was he trying to do? Keep her off? Hardly, as she was safely across the Channel. He was appealing for her sympathy. For the first time he really needed it.

The next year the poor sufferer was condemned to lose all his teeth "but eight pure pearls in front seats" and complained that his chronic angina pectoris was brought on by "the smallest hurry or flurry, acceleration of step or tension."

His last letters to Edith show an informality, a tossing together of slang expressions, Gallicisms, initials and abbreviated words quite unlike his usually carefully organized epistles. The master was relaxing in his use of language for the first time, relaxing with an old and tried and found-to-be-true friend, a pal, really, now that he was free from her motor raids, on whose intense and intelligent sympathy he had come almost to depend.

The outbreak of war, which aroused every fibre of his weakening being in belligerent outrage against the "Hun," provided the final dramatization of the contrast between him and his younger, still feverishly active friend. Whereas Edith was fully engaged in organizing her hostels for Belgian refugees and even visited the front on a hospital mission, James could feel only "like the chilled *vieillards* in the old epics, infirm and helpless at home with the women while the plains are ringing with battle."

When he lay dying, a year later, his secretary kept Edith informed of his condition by almost daily bulletins. I wonder whether any great writer has ever been so admired and loved by another who could hardly read his greatest work. This at last is friendship above art.

Hawthorne *and* Melville

*I*N DECEMBER OF 1850, when Nathaniel Hawthorne and Herman Melville first met in the Massachusetts Berkshires, where the former lived and to which the latter would soon move, Hawthorne was forty-six and the newly famous author of *The Scarlet Letter*. Melville, fifteen years his junior, had also won a degree of fame. His four lively books of seafaring and adventure, *Typee, Omoo, Redburn* and *White-Jacket* (the first two inspired by his life among the Polynesian natives) had enjoyed wide sales. But there was a tragic difference between the destinies that lay in store for the two writers. Hawthorne's reputation, with the appearance in the ensuing decade of *The House of the Seven Gables, The Blithedale Romance* and *The Marble Faun,* would soar until he was generally deemed the finest of American novelists. Melville's, on the other hand, would be so diminished by the masterpiece that he was then in the process of composing, and by its successor, *Pierre,* that in the remaining forty years of his life his name would sink to obscurity. Indeed, not until the 1920s would he be revived and esteemed as an even greater novelist than the older friend in the Berkshires to whom he had so warmly and admiringly dedicated *Moby-Dick*.

It is sad to consider the high hopes of Melville at thirty-one. He had overcome so many hardships: the boyhood poverty made worse because it was the fallen state of a once-grand family, the brutal treatment suffered by seamen on the long, hard cruises of whalers, the near brushes with death at the hands of South Sea cannibals and, perhaps worst of all, the despair of ever having the time or the education to become a writer. And now all was changed: he had money in his pocket from the sale of popular books, a loving bride who was the daughter of the Chief Justice of Massachusetts and a mind throbbing with the germination of what he dared to hope would prove the great American novel!

The two writers were invited by David Dudley Field, the noted law codifier, to join a literary group that climbed Monument Mountain and afterwards adjourned to a shady spot to read aloud the poems of William Cullen Bryant and toast the poet with considerable hilarity over many glasses of Heidsieck. Going home in the late afternoon through the Ice Glen, according to the publisher James T. Fields, "Hawthorne was among the most enterprising of the merrymakers, and being in the dark much of the time, he ventured to call out lustily and pretend that certain destruction was inevitable to all of us ... I never saw Hawthorne in better spirits."

One gathers that it was not a common occurrence for the great romancer, and Melville, who deeply admired his work, may have been both surprised and encouraged to seek his acquaintance. He had just written of him in *The Literary World*:

> Now it is that blackness in Hawthorne ... that so fixes and fascinates me. It may be, nevertheless, that it is too largely

developed in him. Perhaps he does not give us a ray of his light for every shade of his dark. But however this may be, this blackness it is that furnishes the infinite obscure of his background.

But with this blackness at least temporarily in abeyance, the two men at once hit it off. It is not surprising, considering Melville's charm and admiration. What writer, however shy and ordinarily withdrawn, can resist the enthusiasm of a talented junior? Hawthorne not only asked Melville to come and visit him; he proceeded to read the young man's four publications, lying, as his wife, Sophia, described him, "on the new hay in the barn which is a delightful place for the perusal of worthy books." Finishing them, he concluded that no writer had put reality before his reader more unflinchingly, and he and Sophia warmly welcomed their new friend when he came to stay. She wrote to her mother that they found him "very agreeable and entertaining — a man with a true warm heart and a soul and intellect — with life to his fingertips, earnest, sincere, and reverent, very tender and *modest* . . . I am not quite sure that I do not think him a very great man."

Melville was thrilled by their friendship. Whether or not it was what prompted him to buy a farm in the Berkshires and move his wife and baby there we do not know, but it may well have been a factor. His letters to Hawthorne now wax almost lyrical, although he seems already aware of enigmas in the character of the author of *The House of the Seven Gables*. Of this novel he wrote to its author that it put him in mind of a fine old chamber with a fine old desk containing a dark little volume entitled *Hawthorne, A Problem*. He suggested that the grand truth about his friend was that he said No! in thunder, and the devil himself could not make him say Yes! And in a subsequent letter he developed the fancy that they might continue their dialogue in a future state:

If ever, my dear Hawthorne, in the eternal times that are to come, you and I shall sit down in Paradise, in some little shady corner by ourselves; and if we shall by any means be able to smuggle a basket of Champagne there (I won't believe in a Temperance Heaven), and if we shall then cross our celestial legs in the celestial grass that is forever tropical, and strike our glasses and our heads together, till both musically ring in concert, — then, O my dear fellow-mortal, how shall we pleasantly discourse of all the things manifold which now so distress us, — when all the earth shall be but a reminiscence, yea, its final dissolution an antiquity.

I strongly suspect that at this point Hawthorne was beginning to find his exuberant young friend a bit of a strain. We find this entry in his journal on August 1, 1851:

After supper I put Julian [his son] to bed; and Melville and I had a talk about time and eternity, things of this world and of the next, and books, and publishers, and all possible and impossible matters, that lasted pretty deep into the night, and if the truth must be told, we smoked cigars even within the sacred precincts of the sitting room. At last, he arose, and saddled his horse (whom we had put into the barn) and rode off for his domicile; and I hastened to make the most of what little sleeping-time remained for me.

Hawthorne's enthusiasm for *Moby-Dick* reduced Melville to near incoherence: "But I felt pantheistic then — your heart beat in my ribs and mine in yours, and both in God's. A sense of unspeakable security is in me this moment on account of your having understood the book." He almost doubted his own sanity: "But believe me, I am not mad, most noble Festus. But truth is ever incoherent, and when the big hearts strike together, the concussion is a little stunning."

Because of certain suspected difficulties in the marriage relation of the Melvilles and several seemingly homoerotic references in Herman's books to the beautiful bodies of Polynesian males, there have been inevitable speculations that he may have actually been in love with Hawthorne. But to me it seems obvious that if he was homosexual (presumably repressed, as there is no evidence to the contrary), his attraction would have been entirely to handsome, muscular sailors or South Sea islanders, never to such a frail, middle-aged, elegant, intellectual gentleman as Hawthorne — however charming in appearance — seems to have been.

Whatever the nature of Melville's affection, however, it seems clear that it was not returned in anything like the same degree. Newton Arvin, one of Melville's most deeply understanding biographers, finds the beginning of a dryness in the relationship between the two men as early as 1852, only a year before Hawthorne's departure for Liverpool, where he had been appointed consul. It was not that the older man did not like and admire the younger. "He has a very high and noble nature," he wrote of Melville in a later year, "and is better worth immortality than most of us." But as Arvin puts it, Hawthorne was unable to play "the superhuman role — of father, friend, elder brother, and all but God — that Melville, in his misery and egoism, would have had him play."

I suspect that Hawthorne must have found Melville's constant probings into the nature of life and art, and in particular into the nature of Hawthorne's life and art, very trying. The author of *The Scarlet Letter* never wore his heart on his sleeve; indeed, he was a person of the strictest privacy, of an almost impenetrable reserve. This, with the shadowy air of mystery that pervades his tales, has given rise to speculation that something has been concealed. In Academia this speculation sprouts a thousand theories of symbols and ambiguities. Among literary gossips it gives rise to suggestions of sexual repression and even incest. Melville himself, after Hawthorne's death, suggested to Julian that his father had all his life concealed some great secret which, if known, would explain all the mysteries of his career.

Yet the reader of the long, detailed journals that Hawthorne so scrupulously kept during the European years receives no hint of this. They are, like his fiction, beautifully clear and smooth; one feels wafted down a slowly moving river past picturesque landscapes where loveliness is justly appreciated, occasional ugliness (even squalor in ports) conscientiously noted, and history concisely and amusingly supplied. There is no soul searching in these pages, no soul wracking; the passing scene, for better or worse, is calmly delineated, and the universe, of which it constitutes an undecipherable fraction, seemingly accepted. Only where individuals are described does the journalist sharpen his pen to become at times biting; they might be (and perhaps were) portraits that could be later used for characters in fiction. Indeed, the journals might as a whole be the raw material (and not so raw) out of which the tales and novels could be cut.

Then where is the art? Is it simple description of a background, peopled with characters, animated with dialogue and woven together with plot? Well, of course, it is much more than that, but what it is is very hard to say. I can imagine that Melville made himself a magnificent but destructive bull in Hawthorne's delicate china shop, that he picked up piece after piece and demanded to know just how each was put together and just what it was intended to represent. And I am sure this would have been distasteful to the craftsman.

For why is *The Scarlet Letter* a perfect novel? *The House of the Seven Gables* isn't. The reader must deal with its concept of inherited guilt according to his own allegory. *The Blithedale Romance* isn't. The issues between the characters are never clearly defined. And *The Marble Faun* certainly isn't. The faun has his silly side, and the murder is melodramatic. But one would not add or subtract or change a single word of *The Scarlet Letter*. It simply stands there, like a Grecian urn.

But let us be Melville and ask questions. Would Hester Prynne be considered such a sinner in 1850? Consider her story. As a girl she is married off to a rich but old and deformed man. She is taken to a bleak new world, where her husband is captured by Indians, and she is left to her own devices in a colony where she has neither relatives nor friends. A beautiful young preacher, as silver-tongued as he is spiritual, falls in love with her, and she with him, and a child is born of their indiscreet passion. Did Hawthorne consider this so great a sin? Does he not make the point that if it was a sin, it nonetheless created an immortal soul?

It is certain, anyway, that he considered Hester's punishment of permanent ostracism excessive. Well, then, if neither the reader nor the author considers the heroine so dire a sinner, what is the book about? Historical injustice? But there is no attempt to castigate the colonists. Indeed, Hawthorne seems to accept their grim morality. He even seems at times to look back to it with nostalgia.

And Hester, does she not accept her punishment? When she at last flings aside the condemning letter, her daughter picks it up and she patiently dons it again. She seems to accept her shame if not as a judgment, at least as a fact. It is hers; it is *she,* and she has no choice but to live with it.

So what is that? Original sin? Existentialism? Why should she not turn her back on the whole silly colony and seek a new life with her lover?

But the question is just as idle as it is to ask what Cathy Linton can see in such an unmitigated rascal as Heathcliffe. One reads *The Scarlet Letter* for . . . well, I'm never sure exactly what I do read it for, but I certainly read it. Was that Hawthorne's secret? That he didn't have one?

After Hawthorne moved to Liverpool, there was only one more meeting, at least of any significance, between him and Melville. The latter, deeply discouraged by the collapse of his own literary career, decided to try to pull himself together on a solitary trip to Europe, away from everyone, including his wife and children. Passing through Liverpool on his way to the Continent, he briefly looked up his old friend, and they took a long walk by the sea. Hawthorne noted in his journal:

> Melville, as he always does, began to reason of Providence and futurity, and of everything that lies beyond human ken, and informed me that he had "pretty much made up his mind to be annihilated"; but still he does not seem to rest in that anticipation; and I think, will never rest until he gets hold of a definite belief. It is strange how he persists — and has persisted ever since I knew him, and probably long before — in wandering to and fro over these deserts, as dismal and monotonous as the sand hills amid which we were sitting.

A couple of days later Melville departed, and Hawthorne wrote:

> He sailed from Liverpool in a steamer on Tuesday, leaving his trunk at my consulate and taking only a carpet-bag to hold all his travelling gear. This is the next best thing to going naked; and as he wears his beard and his moustache, and so needs no dressing-case — nothing but a tooth-brush — I do not know a more independent personage. He learned his travelling habits by drifting about all over the South Sea, with no other clothes or equipage than a red flannel shirt and a pair of duck trowsers. Yet we seldom see men of less critizable manners than he.

And would not, we regret to feel, care too much if he were not to see him again.

Roosevelt and Hopkins

Richelieu and Father Joseph

The Friendship
of Shared Power

*T*HERE IS always a question as to whether men — and I suppose now we can add women — who have slithered their way up Disraeli's "greasy pole" to its summit of supreme political power are apt to have any real friends. The better question might be: Do they really want them? I doubt that either Napoleon or Julius Caesar did. The former, whose life we know almost from day to day, seems to have been quite content with the company of his own genius. So far as his fellow man was concerned, he could make do with sycophants to amuse him, statesmen to advise him and loyal officers to execute his plans. Power, as is tediously reiterated in literature, is a lonely state. And if it's not, perhaps it had better be. Rare indeed is the friend on equal terms with a chief of state who does not seek some species of advantage from his position.

Such friends do, however, exist, though their rarity makes the public suspicious of candidates when they appear. Or when they don't appear. There is a perhaps defensive move on the part of the ruled to ascribe weakness to their ruler and to see in any hidden palace intimate the true wielder of power, a grey eminence or even a Rasputin lurking behind the throne. But it is still possible to find cases where power has been delegated without any loss of authority to men who merit the title of disinterested friend.

Harry Hopkins may have been the closest that anyone ever came to being an intimate of Franklin D. Roosevelt's. Eleanor Roosevelt wrote, after her husband's death, "I was one of those who served his purpose." FDR had no real confidants, she maintained, certainly not herself. No human being ever fully shared his inner life.

One biographer, Ted Morgan, argues that this was true even from his boyhood.

> He had to fight to get his locks trimmed and to graduate from dresses and kilts. He learned that there was a part of himself he could not reveal to his mother, and acquired an opaque core, a sort of inner armor. It was a matter of survival . . .
>
> It was at his mother's knee that he learned the protective ambiguity that so many of his associates would later comment upon. As the brain truster Rexford Tugwell put it, "He was the kind of man to whom those who wanted him convinced of something — usually something in their own interest — could talk and argue and insist, and come away believing that they had succeeded, when all that happened was that he had been pleasantly present."

After his affair with Lucy Mercer, FDR's relationship with Eleanor became more of a political partnership than a marriage. His children he always loved, but they were usually away and apt to give him more headaches than help, with their divorces and speeding tickets and business problems. Louis Howe — in Kenneth S. Davis's phrase, "that untidy, irritable, asthmatic, chain-smoking little man" — and his secretary

Marguerite (Missy) Le Hand were obsessively devoted to their boss, but idolatry does not make for true intimacy. The President accepted the offer of their lives gratefully, knowing that his success was all the return they looked for. The Brain Trust — Raymond Moley, Rexford Guy Tugwell, Adolf A. Berle, and the others — representing, as Davis puts it, "a historic attempt to bridge the gap between Intelligence and Power," stimulated and excited him, but they were essentially co-workers. As for his social friends, they were for relaxation: Vincent Astor for fishing and yachting, his old college friend Livingston Davis for jokes and drinks and (in earlier days) seeing girls. FDR liked people in quantity, at parties, for banter, for story swapping, for general hilarity.

Yet I suspect he was not lonely; he did not need intimacy. He may even have shunned it. A satisfaction greater than that offered by people may have been supplied by a romantic vision of himself in history, a sense of his destiny that never left him, even in the terrible days of polio, a vision in which America was seen lapped by the blue waves of seas on which rode beautiful naval vessels and covered with rich valleys and streams and productive farms — he was always more of a Jeffersonian than a Hamiltonian, inclined to find the good life in the agricultural countryside as opposed to the wicked city. It was a vision, I suspect, whose setting was reproduced in prints and paintings and stamps, most of all stamps, so clear, so precise, so detailed yet so idealized, affirming America as a peaceful and democratic polity, an America that was waiting for a successor to Cousin Theodore.

This sustained inner identification of himself with the nation could have been a kind of artistic creation. He conformed himself to it, in appearance, in language, in manner, surrounding himself with beautiful and appropriate props: naval paintings and prints, fully rigged ship models, English political cartoons, countless stamps. The knowledge of history that he accumulated was prodigious. Adolf Berle said that he could tell you about naval construction, constitutional law, the story of coins, the ability of white men to live in the tropics — he could tell you about any concrete subject, it seemed, but had little interest in abstract ideas, their analyses, their contradictions. It was only natural that he should turn to people like Howe and Le Hand, who may have glimpsed the vision behind the style. Did any of his family really sense it? How could the verve of his conversations or the brilliance of his speeches have been appreciated by the saintly but humorless author of "My Day"?

It is curious that so hard-boiled a thinker as Harry Hopkins should have shared the vision.

When FDR appointed Hopkins to be chief of the Federal Emergency Relief Administration on May 23, 1933, nobody could have imagined that this was the beginning of a partnership that would ultimately transcend the needs of the Great Depression and provide a vital element of the global force that would bring World War II to a victorious conclusion. Hopkins, whose life had been devoted to social work, to which he brought a blunt, at times brutal honesty, a tough practical common sense and a driving industry, was regarded, with dismay or enthusiasm, depending on one's political point of view, as entirely capable of administering the expenditure of staggering millions in the various agencies spawned by emergency relief, particularly the WPA, but that he should turn out to be a master diplomat and a strategist capable of understanding and implementing global warfare was something that surprised his friends and was never believed by his many enemies. Also, he seemed as different as a man could be from the charming, beneficent Hudson squire in the White House. But Raymond Clapper understood it.

Many New Dealers have bored Roosevelt with their solemn earnestness. Hopkins never does. He knows instinctively when to ask, when to keep still, when to press, when to hold back; when to approach Roosevelt direct, when to go at him roundabout . . . Quick, alert, shrewd, bold, and carrying it off with a bright Hell's bells air, Hopkins is in all respects the inevitable Roosevelt favorite.

And as Robert Sherwood said of FDR's role in the partnership in his splendid *Roosevelt and Hopkins,* the President educated his favorite in the arts and sciences of politics and war and then gave him immense powers of decision for no other reason than that he liked him, trusted him and needed him.

Another important aspect of the friendship between the two men was that Hopkins sensed exactly when the President wanted to work and when he wanted to relax, and adapted himself immediately and entirely to each mood.

When Wendell Willkie once asked FDR why he kept a man so distrusted by many of his constituents so close to him (Hopkins was then actually living in the White House), the President replied:

> I can understand that you wonder why I need that half man around me [an allusion to Hopkins's extreme physical frailty]. But someday you may well be sitting here where I am now as President of the United States. And when you are, you'll be looking at that door over there and knowing that practically everybody who walks through it wants something out of you. You'll learn what a lonely job this is, and you'll discover the need for somebody like Harry Hopkins, who asks for nothing except to serve you.

Hopkins, who, according to Joseph E. Davies, had "the purity of St. Francis of Assisi combined with the sharp shrewdness of a race track tout," had been unfortunate in his health

and in his first two marriages. The damage to his digestive
process caused by the excision of a large cancer in his stomach
had made him a semi-invalid, often on the brink of death; his
first wife had divorced him and his second died. FDR, who
had seriously for a time groomed him to be his successor, was
obliged to give up the idea when Hopkins's health failed to
improve, and also when the war in Europe dictated the necessity for a third term, and Hopkins went loyally to the Democratic National Convention in Chicago in May of 1940 to
spearhead the drive for the nomination.

After this all personal ambition died in Harry Hopkins. He
knew that he could rely on a future only from month to month,
and he dedicated himself heart and soul to the service of his
master. He had resigned the post of Secretary of Commerce,
to which FDR had raised him, and now, at the invitation of
both Franklin and Eleanor (Hopkins was one of the few persons equally close to both), he moved into the White House
with neither a title nor a salary. As Sherwood put it:

> The extraordinary fact was that the second most important
> individual in the United States Government during the most
> critical period of the world's greatest war had no legitimate
> official position nor even any desk of his own except a card
> table in his bedroom. However the bedroom was in the White
> House.

He did receive a salary when he was appointed administrator of the Lend-Lease program to Great Britain, but his real
job was to be always available to his chief for war planning,
except when he was off on exhausting air trips (accompanied
by a watchful navy doctor to make him take his pills) to London, Moscow, North Africa and the Pacific. Winston Churchill often cabled Hopkins directly for his advice before
submitting a project to the President. Hopkins did not move

out of the White House until the summer of 1942, when his third bride understandably wanted a home of her own.

In 1944 he collapsed and was off the job for seven months. After that his relations with the President were much altered. FDR realized that Hopkins was now too ill to sustain the old work load, and fourth-term considerations caused him to soft-pedal his intimacy with a man so unpopular with the more conservative elements of his party. Yes, there was always that side to Roosevelt. But there was no break, as between Wilson and House. The friendship went on to the end. Hopkins survived the President by less than two years. He expressed his faith in his friend to Sherwood in these words:

> You and I are for Roosevelt because he's a great spiritual figure, because he's an idealist like Wilson, and he's got the guts to drive through against any opposition to realize those ideals. Oh — he sometimes tries to appear tough and cynical and flippant, but that's an act he likes to put on, especially at press conferences. He wants to make the boys feel he's hard-boiled. Maybe he fools some of them, now and then — but don't ever let him fool you, or you won't be any use to him. You can see the real Roosevelt when he comes out with something like the Four Freedoms. And don't get the idea that those are any catch phrases. *He really believes them!*

I think one can see the deepest side of the relationship between the two friends in their discussions of a hurricane-proof fishing house that the President wished to build for himself and Hopkins after their retirement on a Florida key. These talks occurred again and again during the terrible tense weeks before the attack on Pearl Harbor. FDR wrote a note to Hopkins, asking him to obtain a "Large Scale Chart of Long Key, Fla. and Channel Key about 3 miles S.W. of it and just off North Side of Viaduct. This is about half way from Key

West to the mainland along the Trestle." The President drew a sketch of the house he wanted and even suggested that Hopkins fly down to the Florida keys to see whether the land could be obtained for a few thousand dollars.

I do not suppose that Hopkins ever thought that the hurricane-proof house would be built. But he knew that the crushing weight of the world crisis rested squarely on the shoulders of his friend and that he might not be able to sustain it without his brief daily periods of relaxation: the chatter in the cocktail hour before dinner, the affixing of stamps in the albums, the half hour in bed with the detective story, the reminiscences told to Hopkins and Missy Le Hand of the old days in Hyde Park. Hopkins, unlike Eleanor with her never-pausing concern for the underprivileged, unlike the New Dealers relentlessly concerned with the loss in war of social objectives, unlike the military men who, quite properly, could never take their eyes from the map, understood how his chief had, before anything else, to be kept alive and alert. And FDR, in his dreams of a shared fishing hut after the war was over, may have showed more affection for Harry than he had felt for anyone else.

I suppose one can always ask about any great man how much that amounted to.

In the Boston Museum of Fine Arts there is a charming small painting by Gerôme, executed with the colorful exactitude of detail that makes French nineteenth-century historical pictures seem like stage sets, representing a scene on a marble stairway of Richelieu's Palais Cardinal. Coming up the steps but pausing to make deep reverential bows to the sole figure descending, a tall, gaunt, bony friar with sandaled feet, utterly absorbed in a missal, is a crowd of richly dressed courtiers. Is the friar really unaware of them, or does the painter imply that his air of holy detachment conceals a heart throbbing with pride at such obeisance to the alter ego of the all-powerful Cardinal Minister? The same question may be raised by *Grey Eminence,* Aldous Huxley's fascinating study of Father Joseph. In his opening chapter, the author imagines the plain, barefoot friar, a dusty pedestrian traveler to Rome, being challenged by the contemptuous papal guards at the Milvio Bridge and producing, in silent obedience, a document of identification signed by His Most Christian Majesty and sealed with the royal arms of France, causing the soldiers to leap to their feet and form a saluting aisle across the bridge through which the impassive priest makes his way, merely raising a hand in blessing.

A consideration of the life of François Le Clerc du Tremblay, however, leads to the conclusion that both artist and author were more concerned with the supposition that Father Joseph *didn't* feel pride than that he did. The most interesting thing about him is that he appears to have totally suppressed his ego or at least converted it into the efficient engine of his conscience. A passionate belief in a crusade to rescue the Holy Land from the infidels had been frustrated when he found the Catholic powers unwilling to undertake it. He then decided that only France could do the job, but that France would first have to be cleansed of her religious civil strife and freed of her containment by the surrounding Hapsburg powers: Spain and the German empire. Both of these objectives had been attained by his death in 1638, and he expired, presumably with the consciousness that part, anyway, of God's plan had been completed. Did he suspect that the crusade would never come about? Perhaps not. His faith in the effectiveness of petitioning prayer seemed infinite.

The great question to us in the twentieth century is how a priest so dedicated could have believed that God would approve the policy carefully worked out by himself and Richelieu of nullifying the aggressive power of the Holy Roman Empire by keeping the Thirty Years' War going as long as they could with money poured into the coffers of Protestants and invading Swedes. The carnage and starvation that devastated the empire was about as horrible as anything history has to offer.

Of course one can understand the strictly nationalistic point of view that would blind the eyes of a statesman to any suffering but that of his own country. But Father Joseph professed to be a mystic. Huxley finds the answer in the friar's having chosen what he calls the "ersatz" mysticism of Cardinal Bérulle. Instead of attempting to annihilate the ego in an imageless godhead, as a true Eastern mystic would, thus freeing himself from nationalism along with all other worldly concerns, the Bérullist sought to lose himself in the image of Christ or even the Virgin. But as the image of Christ was the image of a man, the false mystic had not divorced himself from worldly concerns; on the contrary, he was even more dangerously wrapped up in them, for now any means could be used to justify his supposedly divine ends.

It may have been so, but Huxley is only intelligently speculating. No one can know what went on in Father Joseph's mind in the lengthy meditations that interrupted his constant toil. The student of friendship can only inquire what their effect was on his relationship with the Cardinal.

Religious passion sprouted early in the life of François du Tremblay, a life that had not seemed destined for holy orders. He was born in 1577, the son of a distinguished and prosperous lawyer, the *premier président des requêtes du palais,* and of Marie de La Fayette, of the landed nobility, and he was reared to be a soldier and courtier and to make his way in the great world. His good looks and charm, his intelligence and tact, added to his expert horsemanship and skill with the foils, seemed to promise a fine career. But there were troubling incidents. While still a small boy he had interrupted a family supper party to tell shrilly, with heartbreaking sobs, the story of the Passion. And in his teens he had fallen violently in love with a girl, only to fall just as violently out, stricken with a sudden horror of the idea of the sexual act which was to last for a lifetime. When he was twenty-two it was finally evident to him that he would have to be a priest, and overcoming the violent opposition of his now-widowed mother, he was admitted to the Capuchin order of the Franciscans. So strict were the vows of poverty that it required that in later years, when he was visiting foreign courts as the first minister's secretary of state, he had to seek a dispensation to handle money or ride in a carriage.

The brilliant young courtier was not forgotten, anyway, by astute observers in the royal entourage, and the new Father Joseph found himself assigned to the job of reforming and reorganizing the great abbey of Fontevrault for its abbess, Madame de Bourbon, an aunt of Henri IV. The death of this princess while his work was in progress necessitated many conferences between Father Joseph and Marie de Medici, regent for her young son, Louis XIII, in the choice of a successor. The Queen Mother was a vulgar, stupid and heartless woman, but she was not so stupid as to fail to see that the young friar was a born diplomat, and she remembered him when she needed someone to negotiate peace between herself and the rebellious nobles who had followed the Prince de Condé in his defiance of her rule. Father Joseph managed to terminate the civil war and in the course of his negotiations he met that able and ambitious prelate, the Bishop of Luçon and future Cardinal de Richelieu. When he recommended him successfully to the Queen Mother's service, the great partnership between the two men that was to reorganize France and the face of Europe was launched. It would last without a break, or even a recorded quarrel, from 1624, the date of Richelieu's appointment as first minister to Louis XIII, to Father Joseph's death fourteen years later.

His usefulness, indeed his indispensability to Richelieu, is easy enough to understand. The Cardinal's secretary of state was a man devoid of personal ambition and totally loyal to his master's policy of uniting France under a strong and absolute monarchy and making her the leader of Europe. To accomplish these aims he was willing to work around the clock in his small bare chamber in the Palais Cardinal (or in the magnificent châteaux at Rueil and Richelieu which the Cardinal had erected to his greater glory) and to undertake any number of arduous trips to foreign capitals to negotiate treaties or bribe statesmen. He enjoyed robust health, whereas the Cardinal was always ailing, and he supplied fortitude of character as well. He steeled his chief to the grim task during the seemingly endless siege of the Protestant stronghold La Rochelle, and startled him out of his nervous stupor when in 1636 the Spaniards broke through the French line and threatened Paris from Compiègne. Father Joseph did not know what fear was; he roundly pronounced Richelieu a "wet hen" (then a term to denote cowardice rather than anger) and sent him out to drive unguarded through the streets of the panic-stricken capital to exhort the crowds to volunteer for civil defense.

But what did the always realistic and practical Cardinal think when his trusted assistant, as he undoubtedly did, brought up the subject of his cherished crusade? I have no doubt that he listened tolerantly, knowing that this was something that would never happen and that could always be referred to the future, and I shouldn't be surprised if, on evenings when the two relaxed and discussed literature, in which both took a lively interest, the Cardinal did not allow Father Joseph to read some verses (not too many) from the *Turciad,* the epic poem of 4637 lines that Father Joseph had composed in Latin about a crusade he could at least imagine.

For I cannot believe that Richelieu was not as fond as his cool nature permitted of this strong and ever ready right hand. He called him "my support." I like the way Huxley imagines the way he received the news of the friar's fatal stroke while attending the performance of a play in his private theater.

> Suddenly there was a little stir in the audience. The captain of the guard was bringing a friar, who had something urgently important to say to His Eminence. Richelieu frowned angrily at the interruption, began a sharp phrase of rebuke; then, hearing what the friar was whispering, uttered what was almost a cry of pain and sprang to his feet. The actors were silenced in mid-harangue. Staring open-mouthed into the auditorium, now suddenly alive with lights, they saw the Cardinal hurrying out between two lines of obsequiously bowing and curtseying ladies and gentlemen.

What did Father Joseph feel towards his chief? It may have been that his nature was too absorbed in his own brand of mysticism to have much room left for human affections and that he tended simply to view the Cardinal as the chosen instrument of God's will in fulfilling the destiny of France. But I think he must have liked him as well. People are not generally liked unless they are capable of liking, and Father Joseph consistently, and through every sort of trial, held on to the affections of three persons who were at daggers' drawn among themselves: the King, who put up with Richelieu mostly because he could not afford to dispense with so talented a minister, the Queen Mother, who abominated Richelieu and was eventually exiled by him, and Gaston, Duc d'Orléans, the King's brother and longtime heir presumptive, who spent his life organizing conspiracies to bring about the minister's downfall. Father Joseph, who certainly was no sycophant, must have had more than charm to be liked by all three. His integrity and honesty in human relations had to be strongly apparent, and I think, also, that his Christian love for his fellow men must have spilled over into individual affections.

His schedule was an arduous combination of crowds and solitudes. Here is one day:

4–5 A.M.   Prayers, acts of intention, self-abasement, ado-
            ration.
5–6   Reading of breviaries with his secretary.
6–9   Correspondence about foreign affairs.
9–1 P.M.   Audiences, visits to Richelieu via private stair-
            way. Recess at noon for mass.
1   Dinner: soup and one dish of butcher's meat
            without "ragout or roast," except when he dined
            with the Cardinal.
2–4   Business with the Cardinal or audiences.
4–5   Walk in the garden.
5–8   Dictation of correspondence or dispatches.
8   Supper, followed by a visit to the Cardinal's pri-
            vate apartments for further business unless it was
            a social evening with guests and general conver-
            sation. At last to bed on a thin, hard mattress laid
            on planks, possibly preceded by self-flagellation.

The contrast between the personalities of Cardinal and friar is certainly dramatic. I was tempted to say they had nothing in common but the power they so harmoniously shared, but I am constrained to add that they may have had some of the same faith. One cannot but wonder about Richelieu's faith. Could a priest who made himself the richest man in France after the King, who accumulated a great art collection and surrounded himself with a court, who traveled with an army of guards that broke down the gates of towns too narrow to admit the passage of his huge, luxurious litter, even aspire to Christian humility? Perhaps. The seventeenth century did not find hypocrisy everywhere, as we do. Father Joseph, anyway, may well have believed that his chief was a proper priest. Together they seem to fuse into a single great statesman, one with all the panoply of power, the other starkly simple, one rough and ready, the other neurotically sensitive, both ruthless in carrying out their imagined duty, both morbidly suspicious of women. It might have been better for Europe had they never lived. The ghosts of millions killed in the long wars they sustained would certainly think so.

Arthur Hugh Clough

and

Florence Nightingale

*W*E HAVE SEEN in the lifelong friendship of Hay and Adams a fine, steady example of symbiosis. Yet such a relationship can be tipped to the greater and even exclusive advantage of one partner, in which case it may begin to resemble that of the attracted insect and the closing petals of a carnivorous plant. Lytton Strachey briefly suggested such an ominous friendship, in *Eminent Victorians,* between the poet Arthur Hugh Clough and the great nurse-heroine of the Crimean War, Florence Nightingale. Clough, he claimed, had lost his faith at the time of the Oxford Movement, and had passed his life in a condition of considerable uneasiness, "which was increased rather than diminished by the practice of poetry." It was not until he came under the influence of his wife's cousin, Miss Nightingale, that he developed a sense of something "real."

> His only doubt was — could he be of any use? Certainly he could. There were a great number of miscellaneous little jobs

which there was nobody handy to do. For instance, when Miss Nightingale was travelling, there were the railway-tickets to be taken; and there were proof sheets to be corrected; and then there were parcels to be done up in brown paper, and carried to the post. Certainly he could be useful. And so, upon such occupations as these, Arthur Clough was set to work.

Strachey, who mocked the Victorians to the delight of the Georgians, has fared uncertainly with the second Elizabethans. Subsequent biographers of Queen Victoria have found her a vastly more complicated and difficult sovereign than he pictured, and defenders of Thomas Arnold like to point out that Strachey invented his "short legs." But I once asked Cecil Woodham-Smith whether Strachey's picture of Florence Nightingale had not provided the outline for her own more densely factual biography, and she freely acknowledged that it had. And when I looked into Strachey's source material for his tiny but devastating sketch of Clough, it seemed to me, at least in part, to justify his conclusion. It omitted only Clough's extraordinary charm and talent.

He was born in 1819, the son of a Liverpool cotton manufacturer. It is amusing, in view of the oversized conscience he was later to develop, though hardly important, to note that a family legend maintained a genealogical connection with John Calvin. Business required the Cloughs to move to Charleston, South Carolina, and to reside there during much of the poet's youth, so that when he was sent back to England to attend Rugby School and board with the Arnolds, they became his real family and the famous headmaster his spiritual father.

Clough fell completely under the glowing spell of Thomas Arnold. Strachey may have made an ass of this passionate and muscular Christian, who converted a brutal public school into a kind of theocracy and who urged his boys to seek the acquaintance of the "good poor," but to many of those boys he was nothing less than a god or, as Clough would later write, on Arnold's premature demise, "one of the greatest and holiest men that this generation has produced." But Clough's golden years at Rugby were nonetheless tinged with depression, particularly after three of his intimate friends had departed for Cambridge, leaving him in his last year to deplore the falling off in moral tone of a school deprived of their leadership. Had not his own fallen off, too? He wrote to one of them:

> Indeed after two years of constant and unthought of, and unreproached indulgence, in my burning thirst for praise, do not think me affected or wild in saying that there seems to be an atmosphere of conceit around me enveloping my whole frame like the body does the soul, and that however pure and good my thoughts are when they spring in my heart they cannot come out without passing through and being infected with that.

For such a serious young man to go up to Oxford at the height of the Tractarian controversy was surely a misfortune. That the primary concern of many of the brightest students there should have been transubstantiation, the apostolic succession and the Resurrection may seem curious to a generation more concerned with campus tolerance of sexually explicit posters or the control of "acquaintance rape," but a sampling of Clough's letters to his Rugby friend J. P. Gell (then at Cambridge) may be convincing:

> And it is no harm but rather good to give oneself up a little to hearing Oxford people, and admiring their good points, which lie, I suppose, principally in all they hold in opposition to the

Evangelical portion of society — the benefit and beauty and necessity of forms — the ugliness of feelings put on unnaturally soon and consequently kept up by artificial means, ever strained and never sober.

Concerning the Newmanitish Phantasm, as you term the church, I do not know very much. But perhaps you may be enlightened a little, and even softened by the knowledge that Newman . . . holds the supremacy of *the pure comprehension in and of itself,* but says that submission to a divinely appointed body of teachers and governors, to wit, bishops and presbyters and deacons, is the course that is pointed out to us by the aforesaid *pure comprehension.* [Italicized words are in Greek in the original text.]

Yet there were times when it all seemed too much, even to Clough, and he wrote to Gell that what he really wanted was to get on with his regular courses. If he theorized "only for amusement," he ventured at last to suggest, there might be no "harm in it." But this healthy tendency was more than counterbalanced by the ascendancy gained over him by his tutor, another Rugby man, W. G. Ward, a brilliant and very intense scholar who later went over to Rome, but who at the time was obsessed with questions as to the meaning of biblical passages and the validity of the theological principles of the established church.

This proved at last so upsetting to Clough that he was constrained to impose some limitations on their relationship. One doesn't wonder. On a visit to Rugby for a heated discussion of these same principles with Dr. Arnold, Ward so disturbed his former headmaster that the latter had to spend thirty-six hours in bed. Ward may have finally settled his own problems in submission to Catholic discipline, but he created a dichotomy in the mind of his younger friend that was to last for a lifetime. As the editor of Clough's correspondence, Frederick L. Mulhauser, has written, many who wrote reminiscences of him agreed that Clough's shyness, conscientiousness and inability to act decisively could be explained in terms of religious faith and religious doubt.

After taking his degree in 1841 (he had expended too much energy in theological debates to gain a "first"), Clough became a fellow and tutor of Oriel College at Oxford, where he remained for seven years, constantly tormented by the possible dishonesty involved in his having signed the Thirty-nine Articles of the Church of England, as Oxford then required. In 1844 he wrote to Gell:

> Without the least denying Xtianity, I feel little that I can call its power. Believing myself to be in my unconscious creed in some shape or other an adherent to its doctrines I keep within its pale: still whether the Spirit of the Age, whose lacquey and flunkey I submit to be, will prove to be this kind or that kind I can't the least say. Sometimes I have doubts whether it won't turn out to be no Xty at all.

In 1848 he at last resigned his tutorship, writing to a friend, "I rejoice to see before me the end of my servitude, yes, even as the weary foot-traveller rejoices at the sight of his evening hostelry, though there still lies a length of dusty road between."

Away from soul-tormenting Oxford in the more "real" world of London, Clough became a warden of University College and, later, an examiner in the Education Office. But his major poetic period was over.

Some of the poems that he wrote in his Oxford period and in the ensuing two years are very fine. All the free world listened to the BBC on April 27, 1941, at the low point of Britain's fortunes in World War II, when Winston Churchill ended one of his inspiring addresses by quoting the last two stanzas of "Say Not the Struggle Naught Availeth." There is a dichotomy in Clough's poetry, as there was in his personality, between the sober and sometimes somber musings of religious doubts and the fine free Wordsworthian love of nature, the latter being best expressed in his longest and most popular poem, *The Bothie of Tober-na-Vuolich*.

Reading the latter helps one to see why Clough was so loved by many of the greatest literary men of his day. The nothing-if-not-critical Thackeray hadn't minded owning, "I took a great liking to you." R. W. Emerson was even warmer, writing to Clough about *The Bothie,* "I knew you was good and wise, stout of heart, and truly kind, learned in Greek and of excellent sense," but he confessed that he had not expected a great poet: "Tennyson must look to his laurels!" Matthew Arnold considered Clough his closest friend and wrote the beautiful elegy *Thyrsis* to commemorate him. And one can add to the list Tennyson, Carlyle, Hawthorne, J. A. Froude, Benjamin Jowett, James Russell Lowell, Charles Norton and others, until Clough's friendships seem to read like a roll call of British and American nineteenth-century authors.

It is sad that he did not derive greater joy from the esteem in which he was held. Perhaps the ghost of Calvin was haunting him.

In 1851 the very intelligent and deep-hearted young woman who would marry Clough three years later, Blanche Smith, received a long letter from James Martineau, a Unitarian preacher in Liverpool, in answer to one of hers. She had written to seek his advice on a point that troubled her. Did the conventional English standards of life and character, even when treated by the finest authors, not emerge as unworthy of the greatness of human capacities and the depth of human wants? Was not the spirit of Romantic German literature higher and truer? Martineau answered soberly that German literature was anarchic, that it treated all spiritual phenomena as mere developments of irresistible nature not to be cramped by "ungenial rigor." English literature, on the other hand, at least at its best, showed nature subdued to conscience. And surely that was as it should be?

Blanche must have sighed as she bowed to the pastor's undoubted wisdom. She had heard much of duty and conscience and was to hear much more. Her father was a brother of Florence Nightingale's mother, and her mother a sister of the nurse's father. The Smiths were not as rich as the Nightingales, but they were well off, and Blanche's brother was the heir to W. E. Nightingale's large fortune, as the latter had only two daughters, Florence and Parthenope. But the influence of the Nightingales on their near relations was more spiritual than financial. Florence, at first opposed in her plans to become a nurse, had revealed the crusading zeal and iron character that were to make her name immortal, and her family were soon united enthusiastically behind her. Blanche's mother, the famed Aunt Mai, even followed her niece to Scutari and deserted her family after the war to live with the now-ailing Florence as a companion and housekeeper. Her niece was to "ail" for another half century, during which she would reform hospitals the world over from a furiously productive *chaise longue.* Hers was the apostolic gift to make men leave all to follow her.

But Blanche Smith was to apprehend the seriousness of life not only from her family and James Martineau, but from the man she was to marry. Two months after her receipt of Martineau's letter, Clough wrote to her: "Love is not everything, Blanche; don't believe it, nor try to make me pretend to believe it. *Service* is everything. Let us be fellow-servants. There is no joy nor happiness, nor way nor name by which man may be saved but this." And the very next day he wrote again: "I ask no girl to be my friend that we may be a fond foolish couple together, all in all each to the other."

What seemed to make marriage unlikely, however, at least

for some years, was not a difference of opinion about being fellow servants, but not having enough money. The Smiths were willing to do something but not enough, and Clough had little but his exiguous salary. He resolved to seek his fortune as a teacher and lecturer in America, even though it would involve a long and painful separation, and his letters to Blanche in 1853–1854, largely from the area of Boston, are full of financial estimates and speculations, and well illustrate his inability to come to any sort of decision. They must have been very trying to Blanche, who was smitten by some of his religious doubts (they appear to have been very catching), for she wrote, "It is a sad thing to have so little religion as I have now." To which he simply replied that she should have good hope, that "the only way to become really religious is to enter those relations and those actualities of life which demand and create religion."

Blanche finally put her foot down and advised him definitely to come home and accept the job in the Education Office, which, with what her father now offered, would enable them to marry. He did, and a happy life ensued. Children were born, and his many letters to his American friends show a vibrant interest in everything that was going on, foreign and domestic politics as well as literature and religion.

In Mulhauser's edition of the letters, however, a very different note is suddenly struck on July 12, 1857, with this memorandum:

> I found the new Revise as far as p 64 here — I believe there is more at the post today, but I have not been able to get it — They are so slow that I beg to suggest that you should present the 1st Part, separately. Let it include, say, in addition to what I went through with you, the *Statistical* which I have arranged and send to Harrison's today, and the Army Medical Department.

He is assisting Florence Nightingale in the preparation of *Notes on Matters Affecting the Health, Efficiency and Hospital Administration of the British Army.*

How did it come about? The first mention of the Lady with the Lamp in his published correspondence comes before his American venture in a reply to a letter from Blanche which had evidently expressed her notion of a similarity between her cousin and her beloved. Clough does not seem to have been flattered by the comparison.

> I suppose I am something like "the friend" [Miss Nightingale] in my unsympathetic unloving sort of temper; not so upright perhaps and, I will venture to say, *softer,* in both senses. She is not at all poetical or imaginative or mystical (like me) — *une tête forte,* lucid and not rich, though intelligent; not creative, arithmetical, "positive," matter of fact; a little arid, not tender but of a high steady benevolence — not spiritual; moral, but though not strict, a little hard.

His opinion seems to have soon changed, presumably with marriage and a closer acquaintance with the formidable lady. We know that he accompanied her and her party as far as Calais on her way to the Middle East. And when, after the war, his mother-in-law shut up her town house, sent her husband and daughters to live in the country and moved in to look after her famous niece, believed to be fatally ill from the exhaustion of her nursing duties in Scutari, Clough was in constant attendance. He and Aunt Mai, in the phrase of Cecil Woodham-Smith, became "the twin guardians of a shrine." The biographer further describes their role:

> She [Miss Nightingale] travelled by railway in an invalid carriage attended by Aunt Mai as "dragon" and Clough as courier. Bystanders were struck with awe. She was carried in a

chair, and usually her bearers were old soldiers, who carried her as if she were a divinity. A space was cleared on the platform, curious onlookers were pushed back, voices were hushed, and the station-master and his staff stood bareheaded as she was carried into the carriage. She was already becoming a legend.

Blanche and the children were now sent to live with her father while Clough devoted all the time that he could spare from his job to his duties to the great Florence. It must have been that he saw this as his paramount obligation, the one clear course after a lifetime of doubt as to what a murky deity required of him. And Blanche? We know that her father deeply resented the way Florence calmly helped herself to his daughter and her family, and did not hesitate to blame her for his son-in-law's dangerously exhausted state, but Blanche, to some extent at least, may have been brainwashed by her mother and spouse.

When Clough at length collapsed and had to be sent abroad to rest and recuperate, Blanche (unable to follow him at first because of the children) wrote to him about his friend Sidney Herbert's death, generally believed to have been caused by the same brutal Nightingale schedule of hard work:

> They did not think the journey [from London to Wilton] had made any great difference. He was quite sensible and knew the doctors and took leave of everyone. Sutherland declared that Flo's work in this last six months had not in any way increased the illness, for she only did herself what she gave him to do.

But Blanche would later state that "money-making and working for F. Nightingale" had worn Herbert out. At any rate, travel did not repair whatever was wrong with poor

Clough. His wife went out to join him in Italy when he worsened and was with him when the end came in Florence. He was only forty-three.

And what of the other side of the friendship? Florence's grief was second only to her grief for Sidney Herbert. "Oh, Jonathan, my brother Jonathan, my love for thee was very great, passing the love of women," she wrote. "Now hardly a man remains (that I can call a man) of all those I have worked with these five years. I survive them all. I am sure I did not mean to."

Benjamin Jowett, the great master of Balliol, wrote a very candid letter of condolence to Blanche. He referred to how noble-looking a youth Clough had been "before troubles and cares and false views of religion came upon him." He went on to surmise that the years 1840 to 1846 (the period of her husband's best poetry, though Jowett did not say that) were probably some of the happiest of his life. As these were prior to the advent of Blanche in his life, Jowett had to add, a bit lamely, that his marriage had been a real blessing. He ended, "Tennyson will be much grieved — he was very fond of him."

Oh, those Victorians!

$\mathcal{B}$YRON

and

$\mathcal{S}$HELLEY

HE FAMOUS FRIENDSHIP of the two greatest poets (Keats would make it a trio) of the Romantic era was, paradoxically, more one of minds than hearts. Although occasional mutual distrust and dislike are by no means incompatible with friendship, there was more of both between Byron and Shelley than seems consistent with the term as generally used. Their long and bitter dispute over the custody of Allegra, the illegitimate daughter of Byron and Mary Shelley's stepsister, Claire Clairmont, was not the only thing that soured their relationship. They were opposed in character, habits, temperament and moral outlook. Indeed, it sometimes appeared that the only thing they had in common — yet a strong bond it proved — was their genius. And also, it must be added, their birth. Peter Quennell has put it well in his *Byron in Italy* in the passage describing the first meeting of the two poets in Geneva in 1816. (Byron was twenty-eight and Shelley twenty-four.)

Of his [Shelley's] social origins, however, the traces were clearly marked. Byron was quick to notice — and noticed with gratitude — that Shelley retained the manners of the patrician class and was "as perfect a gentleman as ever crossed a drawing room." Shelley's opinions might be perverse, his clothes might be rumpled and stained and tattered, but he had inherited a grace and a *savoir vivre* that Byron appreciated — envied perhaps, for his own manners were shy and awkward; he had been brought up by a dram-drinking mother in provincial obscurity [though he became a peer at ten]. Not that Shelley would have paid homage to any social law. Indeed, there was nothing that he considered more despicable than the *beau monde* "with its vulgar and noisy *éclat*" — the world from which Byron had so lately fallen and to which he looked back afterwards with such longing eyes — but the effects of breeding and association were still apparent. Glad already, no doubt, to meet a fellow reprobate, another exile cast out by English society, Byron was doubly glad to meet him on the footing of a man of the world, though Shelley himself might be insensitive to their common ties.

From their first meeting to Shelley's death six years later the poets saw each other during only three periods, each of a few months' duration. The first, probably the most mutually satisfactory, was in Switzerland; the second in Venice; and the last, probably the least happy, in Ravenna and Pisa.

Byron in 1816 had already left England for good, pursued by the evil reputation caused by his marital separation, his love affairs, including one with his half sister, and the radical opinions expressed in his nonetheless aboundingly popular poetry. He was a figure so famous that one English tourist matron, encountering him on the roof of Saint Peter's, made her brood of virgin daughters lower their eyes to avoid the devil's glance.

Shelley had not attained anything like the same fame, nor would he until after his death. Of all his works only *The Cenci* enjoyed a second edition in his lifetime. But his leftist political opinions, his campaign in Ireland in the interest of Catholic emancipation, his own proclaimed emancipation from Christian morality as practiced in England, his abandonment of his wife, Harriet, to live publicly with Mary Wollstonecraft Godwin, had given a certain notoriety to this son and heir of a wealthy baronet.

In the spring of 1816 Shelley, eager to get Mary away from the quarrels caused by the importunate financial demands of her father (who proved that beggars could be choosers by demanding cash from his daughter's lover on the ground that a check would disgrace him) for a respite abroad, left England for Geneva, taking their two children and Mary's stepsister. Claire's purpose in accompanying them was a very definite one. She had thrown herself at Lord Byron while he was still in London and had become pregnant. She was determined to pursue him, and that pursuit would last for years. She was naïve in her faith in her own powers of persuasion, but no more so than Shelley in his. He actually wrote to his wife asking her to join him and Mary and become what Quennell dubbed the "platonic apex" of a triangular ménage. "Measured by the yardstick of Shelleyan dogma, the project satisfied every requirement of magnanimous feeling." It is hardly surprising that Harriet felt otherwise. There was always in Shelley an element of the left-wing intellectual baffled by life.

Of course, the first thing Claire did when they arrived in Geneva was to rush to the reluctant arms of her lover and then attempt to fix him to her party by introducing him to Shelley. Byron was much more interested in Shelley than in Claire, and the two men had long and passionate discussions about their shared art. They made a sailing expedition around Lake Lucerne, in the course of which a bad storm almost wrecked their boat, and Byron was impressed by the courage of Shelley, who couldn't swim but who insisted that in case of disaster nobody was to risk his life trying to assist him. But Byron's disgust, when back on land with the women, at Claire's heavy demands on his time and nonexistent affections, and the scathing terms in which he described her to Shelley, convinced the latter that it was time to take his little family home.

Back in England everything went wrong. Harriet Shelley committed suicide, and a court deprived Shelley of all rights over their children. He was hounded by creditors, and it became evident that a removal to the Continent would be a wise course. He and Mary were now married, and Claire had given birth to Allegra. It was decided that the Shelleys and their two children, William and Clara, with Claire and Allegra, should change their domicile to Italy, and the spring of 1818 found the group temporarily settled in Leghorn. Allegra was sent to Venice at Byron's request, and Shelley and Claire followed her in the fall to negotiate with the rich Byron the penniless child's support. Byron refused to have anything to do with Claire, but he was delighted to see Shelley again, and, after laying down the harsh terms from which he never thereafter departed — and which were strictly enforced — namely, that he must have total custody of Allegra in return for her support, he dismissed the subject and took his new friend on tours of Venice to discuss everything in the world but what Shelley had come to discuss. He even offered the Shelleys the loan of his villa in Este, which Shelley accepted.

This was the period of the ride taken by the two poets on the beach at the Lido so picturesquely described by Shelley in *Julian and Maddalo*. The poem has a prose preface with this portrait of Byron-Maddalo, a Venetian nobleman of ancient family and great fortune:

He is a person of the most consummate genius, and capable, if he would direct his energies to such an end, of becoming the redeemer of his degraded country. But it is his weakness to be proud: he derives, from a comparison of his own extraordinary mind with the dwarfish intellects that surround him, an intense apprehension of the nothingness of human life. His passions and his powers are incomparably greater than those of other men; and, instead of the latter having been employed in curbing the former, they have mutually lent each other strength. His ambition preys upon itself, for want of objects which it can consider worthy of exertion . . . His more serious conversation is a sort of intoxication; men are held by it as by a spell.

Shelley, for all his lack of a conventional religious faith, was never cynical like Byron. He had a passionate belief in the infinite capacities of man, once removed from the shackles of conventions and despots, as magnificently enunciated in *Prometheus Unbound*. He was distressed by Byron's black humor, even while spellbound by the brilliance and wit of its expression. And although he did not regard the marriage vow as binding, he took the relations between the sexes with the utmost seriousness and held they should be entered into or withdrawn from only with the deepest feeling and understanding. Witness his offer to Harriet! Indeed, he felt about Byron's fevered and flaunted sex life almost as did the matron on the roof of Saint Peter's.

That Julian-Shelley should be an Englishman and Byron-Maddalo an Italian reflects their different attitudes towards the country in which both had chosen to reside. Shelley cultivated the society of his fellow expatriates and never really adapted himself to the more intimate manners of Italians. He was more conscious of the garlic breath of the Venetian contessas than of their beauty. Like many English tourists, he may have preferred the landscapes and monuments of the peninsula without its inhabitants. Byron, on the other hand, became as

Italian as his new compatriots, to whom he was temperamentally attuned and whose language he learned to speak perfectly. Neither poet in the least admired the other's attitude in these respects.

Byron, furthermore, found Shelley's insularity in other aspects of his personality. He found him naïve and overscrupulous and full of nutty notions, such as his vegetarianism and abstention from wine and liquor. But I believe that the greatest division between the two men was caused by Byron's egotism and selfishness. He had to have his way in everything, and such men, however delightful at social gatherings, tend to be surrounded in their private lives (if they are rich or powerful or famous) by little courts of sycophants who put up with their arrogance for reasons of their own.

Little Clara Shelley died in Este, and the grief-stricken parents decided to get away from the place and spend the winter of 1819 in Naples. Byron wisely advised his friend to drown grief in work, and Shelley later wrote that most wretched men "are cradled into poetry by wrong, / They learn in suffering what they teach in song," lines that surely have a Byronic ring.

Allegra was left with her father in Venice, and the harshness of the latter's treatment of poor Claire must have grown increasingly outrageous to Shelley's mind once a peninsula lay between him and the famous Byronic charm. We find him writing to his friend, the novelist Thomas Love Peacock, that Byron "hardens himself in a kind of inordinate and self-willed frenzy . . . He associates with wretches who seem almost to have lost the gait and physiognomy of man, and who do not scruple to avow practices which are not only not named but I believe seldom conceived in England." He even went so far as to express the hope that Byron's career "must end up soon by some violent circumstance," so that Allegra might be returned to them.

The Shelleys, always restless, moved to Rome, where they lost their little son, William, of a fever, and thence, as Mary could not bear to remain in the site of the tragedy, to Florence, and finally to Pisa. Correspondence with Byron in these years was largely about Claire and Allegra and not apt to improve relations between the poets. When maliciously gossiping friends told Byron that Claire had given birth to a child by Shelley that was put away in an orphan asylum, he believed the story without hesitation, simply commenting that it was "just like them." He also made it clear that under no circumstances would he allow Allegra to return to a household where she might "perish of starvation and green fruit or be taught to believe that there is no deity." Byron never entirely got over the dose of Calvinism he had received as a child, and would assert, half melodramatically, half fearfully, that he knew he was one of the damned. And his disgust at what he considered the Shelleys' fecklessness and irresponsibility was revealed in his crack that they had not been able to raise even one child.

It was, however, the question of Allegra that brought about the next meeting, after a three-year interval, between Shelley and Byron. The latter had regulated his life with his steadier and calmer relationship with the Countess Guiccioli and had moved to Ravenna, where he actually boarded in her husband's palazzo. But the latter rejected the role of complacent husband, and the lovely Teresa was forced to retreat to Florence while her spouse litigated with his tenant, who remained on the premises. Byron at length decided that he had better leave Ravenna, where his association with the Carbonari, opponents of the Austrian occupying authorities, had got him into further trouble, and he invited Shelley to be his house guest and to discuss Allegra's future and his own and Teresa's possible move to Pisa.

Byron's spell at once asserted itself. His household consisted, besides servants, of ten horses, eight enormous dogs, three monkeys, five cats, an eagle, a crow and a falcon, all of whom roamed about and fought in the house. Shelley, enchanted, wrote back to Mary:

> L.B. gets up at two, breakfasts; we talk, read, etc., until six; then we ride, and dine at eight, and after dinner sit talking until four or five in the morning ... L.B. is greatly improved in every respect. In genius, in temper, in moral views, in health, in happiness.

Shelley attributed the change to the new mistress, whom he described two months later to John Gisborne as "a very pretty, sentimental, innocent Italian, who has sacrificed an immense fortune for the sake of Lord Byron, and who, if I know any-thing of my friend, of her and of human nature, will hereafter have plenty of leisure and opportunity to repent her rashness."

He wrote again to Mary:

> Lord Byron and I are excellent friends, and were I reduced to poverty, or were I a writer who had no claims to a higher station than I possess — or did I possess a higher than I de-serve, we should appear in all things as such, and I would freely ask him any favour. Such is not the case. The demon of distrust and pride lurks between two persons in our situation, poisoning the freedom of our intercourse. This is a tax, and a heavy one, that we must pay for being human. I think the fault is not on my side, nor is it likely, I being the weaker. I hope that in the next world these things will be better arranged. What is passing in the heart of another, rarely escapes the observation of one who is a strict anatomist of his own.

Shelley asked Mary to look for a house for Byron and the countess in Pisa, and in due course they were settled in the Palazzo Lanfranchi. In the few remaining months of Shelley's life he saw Byron regularly, talking with him, dining with him, riding with him and engaging in the pistol target practice that they both so loved. He found the companionship of the older poet, whom he now regarded as England's greatest since Milton, "no small relief" after "the dreary solitude of the understanding and the imagination" of his own Italian years. Yet he could write to Leigh Hunt, "Particular circumstances, or rather particular dispositions in Lord Byron's character, render the close and exclusive intimacy with him in which I find myself intolerable to me."

And three weeks before his drowning on the ill-fated cruise with his friend Edward Williams in the sailboat *Ariel,* he wrote to John Gisborne, "I shall see little of Lord Byron . . . I detest all society — almost all at least — and Lord Byron is the nucleus of all that is hateful and tiresome in it."

He even told Harriet Smith (though it was not true) that he was not writing, that he had lived too long near Lord Byron, and the sun had "extinguished the glowworm."

Byron was always very generous in his posthumous appreciations of Shelley, as one feels sure Shelley would have been had he been the survivor. He said once that Shelley was, without exception, "the best and least selfish man" he had ever known: "I never knew one who was not a beast in comparison." But he confessed to Mary Shelley that he had no "genius" for friendship: "I did not even feel it for Shelley, however much I admired and esteemed him."

The two men were too different as poets ever to influence each other in any matter of style, treatment or even subject matter. They did something more important: they inspired each other. Each found excitement and stimulation in the other's genius. They warmed their writing hands, so to speak, at each other's fire. It was something considerably more important than friendship.

Marie-Antoinette

and

The Princesse

DE LAMBALLE

$\mathcal{F}$RIENDSHIP IN ROYAL CIRCLES, particularly between a royal and one who is not, tends to fall into one of two categories: the nonroyal either is totally and tediously devoted to his prince or is a sycophant on the make. Of the second, history abounds in examples, from Sejanus to Disraeli, and as it is not really friendship at all, I turned to the second.

I rejected Jane Churchill and Anna Viroubova as too tedious. The former was the devoted lady-in-waiting to Queen Victoria for fifty years, always in faithful attendance, the "Jane C" of countless entries in the royal journal, a silent and unimportant presence at the meetings of chiefs of state, a mere factor of loyalty, who even died at the same time as her mistress. The second at least had her role, if a nefarious one, in Russian history. She was the stout and colorless young noblewoman who so unaccountably engaged the affections of the last Czarina and repaid her benefactress, albeit all innocently, by arousing the interest of an anguished mother in what the mystic monk, Rasputin, might do for her hemophiliac son.

Anna's story, however, was not unlike that of the Princesse de Lamballe, though her fate was much less horrible. She was arrested immediately after the imprisonment of the imperial family, as Madame de Lamballe was after the invasion of the Tuileries, but she managed to escape to Finland. The rest of her life was a sustained lament for the fate of the Empress, whom she adored as a saint and martyr.

It may merit observation that before sovereigns became figureheads, as they mostly are today, and their families became characters in a kind of soap opera for the diversion of the reading and watching public, it was difficult for anything like a true intimacy to exist between a royal and a nonroyal. As shrewd an observer as Madame de Sévigné said of Mademoiselle de Montpensier, niece of Louis XIII and cousin of the Sun King, that she had got to know her only as well as one could "a person of that rank." And even as late as the 1920s the Grand Duchess Cyril, wife of the Czar Pretender, is supposed to have replied to a person warning her against too close an association with some obvious social climbers in Dinard, "But you see, my dear, to us there's just ourselves and then the rest of you." It was hardly worthwhile to make social distinctions outside the Almanac de Gotha.

There has always been tragedy in the fall from a great position, whether or not fault be involved, even when the fallen has demonstrated incompetence or downright silliness. We forget the inane Richard II of the first act of Shakespeare's play in the dignified victim of the last, and all the follies of Mary Stuart are forgiven in the great grim hall of Fotheringay. It is also the case with Marie-Antoinette in the tumbril in David's cruel sketch and with the swooning Lamballe on the bloody steps of the prison of La Force. The friendship of the two women has been commemorated on thousands of pieces of sentimental porcelain and on medallions on candy boxes, the

Queen shown as handsome, regal, haughty, and her friend as mild, gentle, pale, almost fading away, as if with some dim foreboding of the pikes and feral faces of her fate. Yet it may be right to couple Lamballe's end with her life, for it was by far the most distinguished part of it. Even her friendship with the Queen did not develop into anything more than a sentimental attachment until the October day when the women of Paris marched out to Versailles to capture the royal family and bring them to the Tuileries. It was when the rest of the world abandoned Marie-Antoinette that Lamballe conceived of her real duty as commencing.

The history of the House of Savoy was one of constant intermarriages with the House of France, so it seemed in keeping when, in 1767, a princess who was a cousin but not a daughter of the reigning duke should be wed to a legitimated Bourbon. The Prince de Lamballe was the son of the Duc de Penthièvre and a grandson of the Comte de Toulouse, who was a legitimated bastard of Louis XIV and Madame de Montespan. But illegitimacy, even in that day of blood worship, could be sweetened by wealth. The vast fortune that Louis XIV had forced Mademoiselle de Montpensier to confer upon his first bastard son, the Duc de Maine, as the price of his sanction of her marriage to Lauzun, had ultimately descended to Penthièvre to make him the richest man in France. His son could not have aspired to a daughter of Savoy (William of Orange had spurned the legitimated daughter of the Sun King), but a cousin was within his grasp. That his social status was disputed by many of the old families both then and for generations thereafter is amusingly illustrated by Proust's arrogant character the Baron de Charlus, who might have admitted the Noailles to an equal rank with the Guermantes, "*sauf Toulouse.*" The marriage of Sophie de Noailles to a royal bastard had contaminated even her afterborn collaterals.

Marie-Thérèse de Carignan, like other princesses, was only seventeen when she left her parents and home in Turin forever to become the bride of a young man she had never seen. But at first, for a very brief time, it looked as if her life might be like a fairy story. The prince was handsome and apparently amiable, and he seemed smitten by the blond loveliness and sweet disposition of his Italian bride. His father was widely known as a saint and philanthropist, and his sole sibling, a still unmarried sister, warmly welcomed her new sister-in-law. And there seemed any number of beautiful family châteaux as well as the magnificent Hôtel de Toulouse in Paris.

But Lamballe had already been claimed by vice and disease, and within a year the miserable young man, who had not waited more than a few weeks before returning to his old habits, was dead. The family were kind enough to his childless widow, but she had lost her point in the Gallic scheme of things, and her life was calm but dull in the great houses to which her in-laws rotated in stately turn. She did not even have a fortune to attract a second husband, and her choice was limited, anyway, to princes. Her sister-in-law, Adelaide, would have everything now; Lamballe's death had made her the greatest heiress in France. And it was characteristic of the times that the pious and godly Duc de Penthièvre should, without an apparent qualm, marry Adelaide to the man who had introduced his son to a life of debauchery, the Duc de Chartres, future Duc d'Orléans and the notorious "Philippe Égalité" of the Revolution. What did a few morals matter when it was a question of wedding one's daughter to the son and heir of the first prince of the blood?

After a period of mourning, however, Marie-Thérèse was allowed to take her place in court at Versailles. There was even some idle talk of making her Queen. The aging but ever libidinous Louis XV was now a widower, and there was a faction that dreamed of matching him with a young and virtuous princess before he should become besotted with another venal mistress, but any such hope was dashed by the rising star of the Du Barry. Marie-Thérèse's attention, in any event, was soon absorbed by the new wife of the King's grandson and heir, the lovely sixteen-year-old Archduchess Marie-Antoinette, who was now dauphine.

It is easy to see how readily these two young alien cousins-in-law, the Austrian and the Italian, should have reached out to each other as allies amid the probing stares and half-impertinent flattery of the hard, gilded Gallic court. Marie-Thérèse, pathetic, fragile, widowed and isolated, standing apart from the intrigues and jealousies of Versailles, must have seemed a haven indeed to the young bride, whose lethargic spouse, however inarticulately in love, had been unable thus far to consummate their marriage, whose monarch simply wanted her to be polite to the whore she despised and whose aunts-in-law, daily visited, spiteful and frustrated virgins kept unwed to save their dowries, transparently begrudged her her glittering future.

Happily, this future had not long to wait. In 1774 Marie-Antoinette at twenty found herself with an absolute monarch at her command, his zeal to gratify her every wish compounded by his shame at being so inadequate a bedfellow. And, of course, one of her first demands was that her new and dearest friend should be given an income befitting the favorite of a Queen. For Marie-Thérèse the new Louis XVI revived the ancient post of *surintendante* of the Queen's Household, with all its emoluments and perquisites.

It had been created originally by Cardinal Mazarin to satisfy a rapacious niece and, decades later, discontinued because of the fierce jealousies it aroused. These were revived with its revival. The initial result, however, was not so bad. The Maréchale de Mouchy, nicknamed "Madame Etiquette" by the freedom-loving young Queen, resigned her post of *dame d'honneur* rather than be superseded. But her successor, the Princesse de Chimay, and the Queen's *dame d'atours,* Madame de Mailly, at once began to fabricate ways and means of reducing Marie-Thérèse's new post to a sinecure.

Left to herself, Marie-Thérèse's natural inertia — for she was essentially a passive creature — might have prevented her from defending her prerogatives. And that might have been the best thing that could have happened to her. But she was not left to herself. The Duc de Penthièvre, whose grandmother, Madame de Montespan, had held the post, though for a weak and helpless Queen whose husband she had preempted, felt that his glory was diminished with its diminishment. He appealed to his daughter-in-law's sense of rank — perhaps the strongest sense she had — and insisted that she fight, and as he backed her up with his considerable influence, a victory was obtained.

Alas, it was a Pyrrhic one. Marie-Thérèse had the education and training of a princess and no head nor aptitude for figures or administration. She made a sorry job of running a household of five hundred persons, too indulgent with some, too strict with others, and always overconcerned with ceremony. The harder this conscientious creature forced herself to attend to uncongenial duties, the worse a mess she made of them. Worse still, she persisted in referring disputes to the Queen, whom they bored to death. What was the advantage of being rid of Madame Etiquette if Marie-Thérèse was going to take her place? And did not the latter's stubborn insistence on every last emolument of her office suggest that these things meant more to her than her sovereign's friendship?

Poor Marie-Thérèse, with her bookkeeping and rules and her rather pallid, spaniel-like devotion, was becoming tedious, and the Queen would soon be looking for something gamier.

It is sad to read of her obvious mistakes. Marie-Antoinette adored small gatherings of chosen friends in private apartments at Versailles, free of court formality, and she had accorded her friend a twelve-room flat, perfect for such entertainments. But for these, personal invitations were needed, and Marie-Thérèse insisted that, as a princess of the blood, she could invite people to her apartment only by a public announcement that she would be "visible" at a given time. It is small wonder that Marie-Antoinette preferred the delightful *soirées* in the tiny rooms of a new friend, the Comtesse Jules de Polignac.

Polignac, the tolerant and easygoing husband of the lovely Yolande, had a minor post at court; his wife's exquisite and constant lover, the Comte de Vaudreuil, another. She had little money, but how much did one need to entertain people perishing with ennui? All observers agree about her indolent charm. Her hair was black, as if dipped in ink; her coloring brown; her eyes soft and somber; her manner relaxed and easy; her gait in walking "of a languorous nonchalance." She wore few jewels and the simplest dresses, and she seemed devoid of ambition, intent only on pleasing herself and others. And indeed this may not have been a pose. Many observers have attributed the huge gifts and perquisites that she later obtained to the greed and aggressiveness of her relatives.

In Yolande's apartment was gathered a select group of charming men and women — whose role in life, one might say, was simply to be charming — connoisseurs of elegance in social life, who would exchange witticisms, gallantries and gossip and dance and sing and play parlor games. Marie-Antoinette was enchanted with her new friend and her circle. Soon she and Yolande were inseparable. The two spent their days at the Trianon now, strolling arm in arm in the English garden and along the serpentine stream under the poplars and maples, lunching in the belvedere amid the rosebushes, acting in the evening in the rustic comedies of Marivaux, shepherdesses at noon in the *hameau* and at night before the footlights.

How could Marie-Thérèse compete? Desperately, but with hopeless clumsiness, she endeavored to regain the affections of her wandering friend. She could never learn. When Marie-Antoinette agreed to dine with her at the Hôtel de Toulouse before a ball at the Palais Royal, she found the guests all women, as the strictest etiquette required for widows. One can imagine how soon the Queen slipped away to the better party!

As if this were not bad enough, Marie-Thérèse, jealous of the benefits that flowed to the Polignacs, elevated to duke and duchess, was blind enough to step up her own demands for greater compensation, with the result that she now became associated in the public mind not only with the lesbianism that the ribald freely attributed to the Queen and Yolande, but with the royal extravagance that was depleting the treasury and ruining the country.

There was no chance for a mind trained in feudalism, and a mind, too, that was light and at times inconsequent, in a contest with the mind of a truly eighteenth-century woman trained in a discipline whose first rule was to conceal itself. Could one imagine Marie-Thérèse retorting with tranquil impudence, as Yolande did to the Queen when the latter objected to certain new faces in the Polignac circle, "Does Your Majesty's gracious pleasure in my salon require the exclusion of my friends?"

Marie-Thérèse fled the sneering court, where she was only half defended by the Queen (though the latter, essentially good-hearted, would not hear of her giving up her office) and took such intense refuge in illness, whether real or imagined or both, that her life was at last despaired of by her doctors, who, oddly in that benighted chapter of medical history, had not already succeeded in killing her. But at her brother-in-law's she encountered a Saxon physician, Saiffert, who seems to have been a kind of early psychiatrist and who experimented with drugs. When his treatment restored her health, his very life was threatened by rival doctors, who wanted to get rid of the "foreign quack," and when he accompanied his patient to England for a cure of sea bathing at Brighton, the rumors that they were lovers were for a time credited by the Queen herself, who wrote to Marie-Thérèse to send her doctor away. One can only hope the rumors were true.

The emigration, with the advent of the Revolution, of so many of the royal family and their friends, including the whole of the Polignac clan, brought Marie-Thérèse back to her old friend, who was now glad enough to see her. Help was welcome in reorganizing the vast and dirty Tuileries, which had not been occupied for more than a century, and one can imagine that Marie-Thérèse, free of the snickers of Marie-Antoinette's fair-weather friends, may have gone to work with something like efficiency. But she did not find herself taken back into anything like the early intimacy. Marie-Antoinette, who had grown serious and political in the crisis of the monarchy, regarded her friend as too frivolous to be consulted in the plans she was now concocting or in the secret messages she was sending to political leaders. Besides, had not Marie-Thérèse refused to renounce her brother-in-law, Orléans, whom the Queen regarded with loathing as one of the prime causes of all her troubles? Could she be trusted not to reveal important matters, if only by indiscretion, to that traitor to his class and family?

Once again Marie-Thérèse found herself idled. When the Marquise de Lage returned to court, she improvised for her a *jolie toilette* and took her to a gathering at Lady Kerry's, where the remnants of the fashionable world still met, assuring her

that Paris was not nearly "so terrible or frightening" as was
thought in the provinces. But the bitterest blow came when
she was notified of the flight of the royal family in June of 1791
by Marie-Antoinette's letter, delivered after the departure. She
fled herself now to Brussels, presumably determined not to
return until the King and Queen should re-enter Paris at the
head of an Austrian-Prussian army to put an end to the vio-
lence of the Revolution.

At the news of the capture of the royal family at Varennes
and their humiliating return as prisoners to the capital, Marie-
Thérèse underwent the greatest crisis of her life. Everyone
around her told her it would be folly to go back to Paris. And
indeed it had been one thing to join the Queen in the Tuileries
in October of 1789, when the bloodshed was still only sporadic
and there seemed a fair chance of establishing a constitutional
monarchy, but it was quite another now, when the royal family
were incarcerated in their own palace and hooted on the rare
occasions when they were allowed to drive out, and when
political leaders were shouting for the deposition of the King.
But Marie-Thérèse, in full awareness that she was risking her
life, decided that her duty required her to return. Her friendship with Marie-Antoinette, however tattered, was the only
thing that seemed to make any sense of her sad life.

But that friendship was now at last cemented. Marie-Antoinette finally understood and fully appreciated the quality of
devotion that Marie-Thérèse brought to her in her terrible
trouble and loved her in turn. From now on her friend was
fully included in the intimate life and secret plans of the royal
family. It has even been claimed by minor historians that she
constituted a link between the Queen and some of the *enragés*
in the former's desperate last-ditch effort to work out some
kind of a compromise, but I can as easily see Anna Viroubova
closeted with Lenin in the Winter Palace, or Lady Churchill

dropping in to the reading room of the British Museum to confer with Karl Marx, as I can see Madame de Lamballe receiving Danton or Robespierre in her apartment in the Pavillon de Flore.

But what is sure is that Marie-Thérèse demonstrated a courage that she had never shown before. When the howling mob invaded the Tuileries in June of 1792 and hurled their insults at the Queen and her children barricaded behind a table, it was the woman who had once fainted at the sight of a lobster who was now willing to interpose her body between her mistress and the would-be assassins. "The greater the danger, the greater is her strength," wrote Madame de Rochejaquelein of Marie-Thérèse. "She is ready to die; she fears nothing." And on the hot August morning of the final assault on the palace, listening through the vast open windows to the tocsins sounding over Paris, Marie-Thérèse calmly replied to a woman who suggested that all might yet be well, "My dear, my dear, nothing can save us now." And then she went to take her place by the Queen.

When the royal family were sent to prison in the Temple, Marie-Antoinette begged that Marie-Thérèse be allowed to accompany them as a member. The request was denied, and Madame de Lamballe was sent to the prison of La Force, where she was slaughtered in the September massacres. Tried by a kangaroo court, she was given one last mock chance. Would she swear her loyalty to liberty and equality and her hatred of the King and Queen? To the first two she agreed, but to the last she could not. What sense would her life make if she were to swear a hatred of Marie-Antoinette?

Shortly afterwards the Queen fainted at the sight of her friend's severed head raised to her prison window on a pike.

$\mathcal{E}$MERSON

and

$\mathcal{T}$HOREAU

A Friendship
of Shared Style

$\mathscr{H}$ENRY DAVID THOREAU, graduating from Harvard in 1837 at the age of twenty, went straight home to his native Concord and stayed there, quite contentedly and with few absences, for the remaining twenty-five years of his short life. He never married, or engaged in any business, including the modest family one of making pencils, more than was necessary to eke out a simple existence primarily dedicated to the study of nature in his immediate environment and its incorporation into beautiful prose. He was short and plain, "ugly as sin," according to the probably exaggerating Hawthorne — the only two big things about him, it was said, were his nose and his ideas — and possessed of a sensitive and prickly disposition. But he could get more, in the quip of Clifton Fadiman, out of ten minutes with a chickadee than most men could get out of a night with Cleopatra. To quote Hawthorne again: "It may be well that such a sturdy, uncompromising person is fitter to meet occasionally in the open air than as a permanent guest at the table and fireside."

A more sympathetic man, and one who at once perceived the genius of this earnest youth and proceeded promptly to take him on as a friend, protégé and pupil, was his neighbor Ralph Waldo Emerson, fourteen years his senior and already a nationally known lecturer and essayist. Does literary history have any parallel of such immediate recognition by an old light of a new? Emerson totally sympathized with this odd young man's unconventional plan to preserve himself for the study of nature and took him into his own home, supporting him in return for a few handyman's chores. After two years, during which Thoreau was at liberty to roam the countryside ("I have traveled much in Concord" was his famed later remark), Emerson decided that he needed broadening and sent him down to New York with a job as tutor to the children of his brother, William Emerson. But Thoreau was never happy away from Concord, and 1843 found him back there for good.

What was his attitude to so loving a benefactor? The references to Emerson in his journal are few, and the later ones are not all complimentary, but one in these first years asserts that "more of the divine was realized" in the Sage of Concord than in any other man. Gratitude, I suppose, is a tiring burden, and idolization is not always affection. Thoreau seems to have been fonder of the austere Lydian Emerson (with whom her husband, despite their progeny, wrote that he lived like a bachelor). He may even have been inarticulately in love with her.

The real bond between the two men was the art, which the younger must at least in part have learned from the elder, of the sentence. That the sentence is the unit of prose composition is obvious enough, but with these two writers it was a unit that could stand by itself, so that their essays form a series of apothegms, sometimes only lightly strung together. I offer only two of the best known examples: from Emerson, "Society everywhere is in conspiracy against the manhood of every one of its members," and from Thoreau, "The mass of men lead lives of quiet desperation."

The need to hammer observed experience into the limits of perfectly balanced subjects and predicates is conducive to journal keeping, and both men did so on a giant scale. Thoreau recognized explicitly what he was doing.

> Sometimes a single and casual thought rises naturally and inevitably with a queenly majesty and escort . . . Fate has surely enshrined it in this hour and circumstances for some purpose . . . Shall I transplant the primrose by the river's brim to set it beside its sister on the mountain?

In this respect Thoreau resembles La Rochefoucauld, and it is a very important respect, for I believe that the maxims were as important to the duke as his battles or court visits, and the apothegms of the hermit of Walden of a value to him equal to the lake and its denizens.

What is astonishing about both Emerson and his pupil was the vast continents of art and literature that were closed to them. Neither had the least use, to begin with, for the tales of Hawthorne, their close friend and neighbor. Henry James found in Emerson "an insensibility ranging from Shelley to Dickens and from Dante to Miss Austen, and taking *Don Quixote* and Aristophanes on the way." And when he guided the seer on a visit to Paris in 1872 through the galleries of the Louvre, he was struck "with the anomaly of a man so refined and intelligent being so little spoken to by works of art." Thoreau could see nothing but frills in the adornments of architecture:

> What if an equal ado were made about the ornaments of style in literature, and the architects of our Bibles spent as much time about their cornices as the architects of our churches do? So are made the *belles-lettres* and the *beaux-arts* and their pro-

fessors. Much it concerns a man, forsooth, how a few sticks are slanted over him or under him, and what colours are daubed upon his box.

But this is surely disingenuous. Thoreau spent just as much time and care developing his style in the thousands of pages of his journal as did any of the artists he so derides. Does he not say on a later page that "a written word is the choicest of relics," and add approvingly that Alexander carried the *Iliad* with him on his expeditions in a precious casket? It ill became him, who had only to take pencil and paper to the wilderness, to label as slaves of Mammon those who required bricks and marble.

Emerson was the greater artist. His essays contain some of the most beautiful language in our literature. How Henry James could have thought he had never developed a "style" is to me one of the mysteries of criticism. Thoreau in *Walden* comes close to the master, but he falls behind in the homeliness of his details and in the occasional smugness of his heavy satire. It almost seems as if he were reacting against the chiseled beauty of Emerson's prose. The latter's sentences were so fine that he needed nothing else. They became, like marble statues, part of the garden that was Concord. Their composer, serene, calm, detached, bland in speech and manner, the soft-spoken philosopher revered by all, did not often trouble himself on his strolls in the woods and along the river to pluck flowers or feed squirrels or even to identify the different species of flora and fauna. As Thoreau observed, he wouldn't have been willing to trundle a wheelbarrow through the streets of Concord because it would have seemed out of character. Emerson communed with nature on a spiritual level, using his eyes to take in the landscape and his lungs the fresh air. He had no need to brace himself with cold or rain or spend the night under the stars. He had a comfortable, well-appointed home, a well-stocked library, a crackling fire and a household to tend to his needs.

It may have been in partial rebellion against all this that Thoreau conceived his plan in 1845 of moving into a one-room cabin, built with his own hands by Walden Pond on some of Emerson's land. There was a wildness in his nature that was constrained by the elegance of the master's way of life. He needed a more direct affinity with the out-of-doors; he had to "live," as he put it, as well as write, or possibly to live in order to write. He never advocated the life of the hermit, nor did he even claim to be one; in his two years at Walden he made almost daily trips to the village and brought back his necessities. He made it perfectly clear that what he was doing was for himself alone, to satisfy his need to live more fully and happily by reducing to a minimum his dependence on commercial civilization and emphasizing his essential relationship to other animals. And, of course, to write a book, a beautiful book, about it.

Emerson, long before his intimacy with Thoreau, had almost uncannily predicted just what this book would be:

> If life were long enough, among my thousand and one works should be a book of nature whereof Howitt's *Seasons* should be not so much the model as the parody. It should contain the natural history of the woods around my shifting camp for every month in the year. It should tie their astronomy, botany, physiology, meteorology, picturesque, and poetry together. No bird, no bug, no bud, should be forgotten on his day and hour.

The years at Walden did not end the friendship between the two men, but they ended the early intimacy. There were even now occasional notes of a mutual exasperation in their journals. In 1853 Thoreau recorded: "Talked or tried to talk with R.W.E. Lost my time — nay, almost my identity." And three years later we find this entry of Emerson's: "If I knew only Thoreau, I should think co-operation of good men impossible. Must we always talk for victory . . .?" One can picture the stubbornly insisting, at times the almost churlish younger man and the bothered but still bland older one, who preferred lectures to heated discussions, yearning for a converse more civil, more sedate.

But it may be significant that Thoreau wrote of almost losing his identity. That had always been the danger in the old friendship, to be lulled by honeyed words into a life that was too purely one of the mind. Thoreau had conceived in an early essay on friendship of a spiritual union of two souls rather too ethereal to be achieved on earth, and now he appeared to renounce it. He wrote in *Walden* that he had three chairs in his hut, one for solitude, two for friendship and three for society. It began to seem that he would need only one:

> What was the meaning of that South Sea Exploring Expedition, with all its parade and expense, but an indirect recognition of the fact that there are continents and seas in the moral world, to which every man is an isthmus or an inlet, yet unexplored by him, but that it is easier to sail many thousand miles through cold and storm and cannibals, in a government ship with five hundred men and boys to assist one, than it is to explore the private sea, the Atlantic and Pacific Ocean of one's being alone.

But the exploration of that private sea is still worth it: "Every man is the lord of a realm beside which the earthly empire of the Czar is but a petty state, a hummock left by the ice." And the famous aphorism with which Franklin Roosevelt heartened the nation in the depths of the Great Depression was inspired by this entry in Thoreau's journal: "Nothing is so much to be feared as fear."

Fitzgerald

and

Hemingway

If This
Be Friendship . . . !

F. SCOTT FITZGERALD and Ernest Hemingway were near opposites in both their inner and outer natures. Fitzgerald at thirty had enjoyed too much success too soon. In France, he and Zelda wasted their lives in parties and liquor. Drunk, as he was too much of the time, he was impossible. He engaged in outrageous pranks, flung drinks and ashtrays about the room and was appallingly rude not only to fellow guests but to servants. Such things seem peccadillos to later generations of admirers, not so to contemporaries. I once asked his Princeton classmate Hamilton Fish Armstrong, the renowned commentator on foreign affairs, about him. "He was as boring as any other drunk," he told me. "Perhaps a little more so. I gave up trying to see him. What was the use?"

And yet the sober Fitzgerald could be a man of great charm, the charm of a generous and affectionate nature. There was something innately lovable about him. The same could not be said of Hemingway, whose hard head could carry any number of drinks, but who concealed beneath an affable manner and a seeming warmness a cold heart and a jealous ego.

When the two met in a bar in Paris in 1925, Fitzgerald, three years the senior, was already famous; Hemingway was poor and struggling. Yet Hemingway had by far the stronger personality; he immediately took the lead in the relationship, which I find hard to call a friendship. A letter that he wrote to Fitzgerald two months later shows that he had already established the superiority of the he-man to the inebriate:

> I wonder what your idea of heaven would be — a beautiful vacuum filled with wealthy monogamists, all powerful and members of the best families, all drinking themselves to death ... To me heaven would be a big bull ring with me holding two barrera seats and a trout stream outside that no one else was allowed to fish in and two lovely houses in the town, one where I would have my wife and children and be monogamous and love them truly and well and the other where I would have my nine beautiful mistresses on nine different floors.

How could Fitzgerald not see through the crassness of the pose? But he didn't. At least not at first. When the more imaginative Zelda called his new friend "a pansy with hair on his chest," he was distressed. I do not mean to imply that her description of Hemingway was accurate, simply that it was a fitting retort to his self-inflation. But Fitzgerald's admiration of virility in men and doubts about it in himself (as in his asking Hemingway's opinion of the size of his penis in *A Moveable Feast*) inclined him to accept Hemingway's evaluation of Hemingway, and that his new friend should be a great writer to boot completed his enslavement.

It is rare for writers of the first rank to feel no jealousy of each other. Gore Vidal put it aptly when he told me that, reading a rave review of a friend's book, he always "died a little." But there are exceptions. Shelley seems to have been one with Byron, and Fitzgerald certainly was with Hemingway. Glenway Westcott wrote after Fitzgerald's death in 1941:

> [Fitzgerald] not only said but, I believe, honestly felt that Hemingway was inimitably, essentially superior. From the moment Hemingway began to appear in print, perhaps it did not matter whether he himself produced or failed to produce. He felt free to write for profit and to live for fun, if possible. Hemingway could be entrusted with the graver responsibilities and higher rewards, such as glory, immortality.

And Hemingway was quite willing to be entrusted with these things. According to Kenneth S. Lynn, whose *Hemingway* is in my opinion the profoundest study of that great writer and greater egotist, Hemingway, long after Fitzgerald's death, when the latter's posthumous glory threatened his own supremacy in American letters, revised his opinion of his friend downwards and condescended to his memory. Here is what he wrote to Arthur Mizener:

> He was romantic, ambitious, and Christ Jesus, God knows how talented. He was also generous without being kind. He was uneducated and refused to educate himself in any way. He would make great studies about football say and war, but it was all bull-shit. He was a charming cheerful companion when he was sober although a little embarrassing from his tendency always to hero-worship . . . Above all he was completely undisciplined and he would quit at the drop of a hat and borrow someone's hat to drop. He was fragile Irish instead of tough Irish.

Hemingway was to continue his subtle denigration in *A Moveable Feast,* contrasting, as Lynn puts it, Fitzgerald's nervous volubility and femininity with the easygoing manner of

186 / LOVE WITHOUT WINGS

the manly fellow who was with him. He has nothing to say about all the help he had received from Fitzgerald in promoting his career or of the excellent advice (which he had taken) to cut the opening chapter of *The Sun Also Rises*. As Matthew Bruccoli, Fitzgerald's most nearly definitive biographer, says, "Hemingway not only took Fitzgerald's advice about cutting the novel, but decided it was his own idea."

After their initial intimacy in France and Fitzgerald's return to the United States, they saw each other only infrequently, though they occasionally corresponded and certainly never lost sight of each other. Hemingway now became world famous and seemed more than ever the captive of his own silly role of professional tough guy, while Fitzgerald's career, hampered by alcoholism and Zelda's declining mental state, went from bad to worse. Hemingway, who detested Zelda quite as much as she did him, believed, perhaps rightly, that she was maniacally jealous of her husband's genius and intent on destroying him by encouraging his drinking and agonizing him by taking lovers of both sexes. If ever a man paid a heavy price for an obsession with masculinity, it was Scott. Hemingway and Zelda seem like two Furies whose mission was to vent on a sexually insecure Orestes all the wrath of the he-man and the she-woman.

Hemingway's famous and cruel introduction into "The Snows of Kilimanjaro" of a disdainful reference to "poor Scott Fitzgerald's" romantic awe of the rich brought a protest from the author of *The Crack-up*. "If I choose to write *de profundis* sometimes," Fitzgerald wrote with a fine dignity, "it doesn't mean I want friends praying aloud over my corpse." Hemingway's response Fitzgerald destroyed, but not before showing it to a friend, who later described it as written in language "you'd hesitate to use on a yellow dog." Fitzgerald was at last clear about his supposed friend. He observed of him that he was quite as nervously broken down as he, Fitzgerald, but that he manifested it in megalomania rather than melancholy.

As both Margaret Chanler and Edith Wharton are considered in these essays, I venture to repeat an anecdote that Mrs. Chanler told me about Fitzgerald that I have printed elsewhere. We know the famous episode of Fitzgerald's calling on Mrs. Wharton when he was drunk and telling her that he and Zelda were staying in a bordello. She responded coolly by asking what a bordello was. Of course, she knew; her question was an effective put-down. But there was a follow-up. Fitzgerald regretted his boorishness. He told Mrs. Chanler, whose son Theodore was a friend of his, that he had three ambitions in life: to be faithful to Zelda, to write the best and clearest prose of the twentieth century and to become a friend of Edith Wharton's. Mrs. Chanler responded that the first was too personal for her to comment on and that she wished him good luck on the second. But her answer to the third was: "I can tell you right now, young man, that you are going to have to cut down on your drinking if you ever hope to become a friend of Edith's!"

Would that he had. But I, for one, believe that the second wish was granted. And that the spirit of Hemingway is scowling at him in the Hall of Fame.